Drama Queen

Hollywood to Olympus Book 2

Elle Rush

ISBN: 978-0-9939904-1-0

.

Blurb

Layla Andrews isn't really a bitch – she just plays one on television. For the last eighteen months, she's acted like one in real life too while she was forced to serve probation for something she didn't do. Now the Queen of Olympus has done her time and she's ready to start living again…but she's forgotten how.

Russ Vukovich, the show's fight coordinator, had been attracted to Layla since the first time he saw her. Recently he's caught glimpses of a new side of her – one that makes her irresistible. But as he gets closer to her, he also sees more of what she hides beneath the mask she wears.

As Layla and Russ try to navigate their new relationship, families, danger and secrets work against them at every turn. Can they find a true happily-ever-after when they are surrounded by lies?

Dedication

Thank you to my sister, who convinced me to finally take the leap. And thanks to everybody at the office who said "That is so cool!" when I told them I was quitting the corporate life to write full-time. It's a lot easier to chase my dream knowing I have people who are cheering me on.

Acknowledgements

Thanks to Barb and Jenn for their excellent input, and to Holli and Drew for their continuous encouragement.

Chapter 1

It was a top down, wind in her hair, cruising kind of day. The fact that it was raining, the convertible's top was firmly raised, and she was stuck in traffic did nothing to diminish Layla Andrews' good mood. Freedom was in the only slightly smoggy Los Angeles air and she was breathing it in for the first time in ages.

Layla beamed at the security guard who waved her through the studio gate. Even after two years, he still looked at her like he didn't know her until she lifted her sunglasses and he saw her face. Then he couldn't lift the gate fast enough.

She cruised the busy throughways until she pulled into her personal parking spot outside the small soundstage with the Olympus logo on the side. It had been home for a while now but this was the first time she stopped to really look at it. This was the place that had made her famous as Hera, queen of the Greek gods, and television wife to the hottest man on television. Getting that role had been the best and worst day of her life. Today was the day the scales started to tip back towards the good side and she was going to do everything possible to keep that momentum going.

When the show began almost two years ago, it was one more cable show tucked in among all the others that was thankful for a first season of thirteen episodes. Then it went to air and the world fell in love with the Olympians and their assorted love affairs, wars and tragedies. The second season started with a bang and the show's popularity exploded exponentially. Today was a non-filming day for the second episode of season three.

Layla snatched the script off her passenger seat and double-checked the dialogue she had to learn for the week. With her face in the pages, she didn't notice the crack in the pavement just outside her car door. Her toe caught on it and she stumbled as she stepped out of her car. A pair of muscular arms kept her from hitting the pavement.

"Careful, Miss Andrews," a growly voice whispered in her ear.

Layla didn't try to stop the shiver that went down her spine. Some women were about the chest or the butt or the face. To be honest, any of those aspects could be appealing. But Layla had two weaknesses, and arms like the ones around her were the first. The deep voice like the one speaking to her was another. In the abstract, they got her every time. These arms and this voice in particular...she was lucky their owner kept her from falling as she went weak in the knees.

She got her high heeled boots tucked underneath her and tried to stand again. She looked into his light brown eyes and smiled. "Thanks, Russ," she said as she patted his chest. His deeply tanned skin was warm to the touch through his cotton shirt.

The show's fight coordinator held her a moment longer before letting her go. "You're welcome, Miss Andrews. You're early this morning."

"I have to stop by Hair and Make-up."

"I won't keep you then. Have a good day."

Layla stood in the parking lot, staring blankly at the logo on the wall again as she tried to remember where she was going. Once Russ's muscular legs vanished around the corner of the building, her brain managed to reboot. She had a consult with her stylist before the table read. She flipped through the rest of the pages to make sure she'd be working with Russ again. The extra hours of training made days incredibly long but working with the show's fight coordinator was something she never complained about.

She passed a roving security cart as she headed to the hair and make-up trailer, which was a few doors down from hers, separating the stars from the recurring and guest actors. A flood on the soundstage two weeks before filming began for the season had everything topsy-turvy. The main sets had survived but everything else had been moved to portable trailers. Layla knocked on the door and when she didn't get a response, she pushed it open and went in.

The stylist she saw most often was Erin Thorne, and the woman was in the trailer. The busty blonde hadn't answered because she was too busy crawling around on her hands and knees, groping for a little packet of white powder that had fallen under one of the styling chairs. A small pile of similar packets sat on top of a manila envelope on the seat of the chair. Color her shocked. Despite Layla's regular icy demeanor, such things couldn't be kept secret for long in a stylist/client relationship and she'd never seen the woman high or even heard her talk about drugs.

"Oh, shit!" Erin cried. She stood too quickly and cracked her head on the steel underside of the chair, the thump loud enough for Layla to hear. "Shit, I am so fired."

Layla didn't have a chance to answer her before a flush came from the tiny bathroom in the back. The thin door opened and an acne-scarred man in a golf shirt and slacks stepped out. He didn't bother to look at who he was addressing when he announced, "We're in a meeting. Get out."

Despite her personal problems since getting the role of Hera—of which she'd had plenty—Layla had been one hundred percent professional on the job. She knew the name and face of every cast member, crew member, production staffer and studio person that worked on Olympus or who had ever come onto the set. She might not bother talking to them but she recognized them. This guy wasn't one of her people so professional rules did not apply.

Her good mood chilled and the unamused look she'd worn as a shield for so long slid back into place. "Try that again."

"Listen, bitch—"

Layla threw the trailer door open. "I need security in here!" She left it open and pointed to the drug stash. "Is that his or yours?" she asked Erin.

"His."

"You have about fifteen seconds," Layla informed him.

The guy scrambled to jam the baggies into his coat pocket. He still had the envelope in his hand when a pair of security guards arrived at the door.

"Is there a problem, Miss Andrews?" the taller one asked.

"I don't think he has clearance to be here. Unless he was with you, Erin?" Layla looked at the shaking hairdresser. "Is he your boyfriend?"

Erin shook her head and swiped a tear from her cheek. "He won't leave."

"I can take care of that." Layla stared at the guards. "He'll be leaving the lot now, gentlemen. Thank you." One took the skinny man's arm and the other pulled the door shut behind them.

Erin collapsed into the chair and her tears started falling in earnest. "I'm sorry, he's my ex-boyfriend. I haven't seen him in months and then the gate called to say he was here to see me and he owes me money so I thought he was finally coming to pay me back," Erin babbled. "Then he tells me he's going to pay me in H because he knows there's a demand on set and you walked in and now I'm broke and fired."

The tears flowed faster and were joined by shoulder-shaking sobs. Layla had no idea what to do, but she knew all about a person's past sneaking up and ruining everything. She picked the tissue box off the counter and held it out. Erin grabbed a handful of tissues and tried to blot her face. "When did you get fired?" Layla asked.

"You aren't going to fire me?"

"You don't work for me."

Erin sniffled. "I might as well. If you file a complaint, I'm out of here. All because of Dickhead Jeremy."

"Did you lie to me? Were those drugs yours?"

"No."

"Are you using?"

"No! Why do you think I dumped his ass?" She stared at Layla and her breathing evened out a little. "Are you saying you're not going to say anything?"

"If I ever see you with drugs again, I will. Or if you invite your ex back. For this, no. It wasn't your fault. I don't think you should be punished for it."

Layla braced as Erin launched herself at her. "Oh, thank you, thank you."

With her arms pretty much pinned to her side, Layla awkwardly patted the woman on the back. She wasn't the touchy-feely type. At all. "It's fine." It took a few more pats before Erin released her. "Is he going to cause you any problems since I got him tossed out of here?"

"I don't think he's that stupid."

"Never underestimate the potential of stupid." It

would bite you in the ass every time. "Do you want me to talk to security at the gate?"

This question earned her another hug, requiring more back patting. When Erin let her go in a rush, Layla fell into the chair and tried to catch her breath.

"Why are you even here?" the stylist asked her.

Layla grabbed the thick black braid that fell down to her waist and hauled it over her shoulder. "We were supposed to talk about an up-do you wanted to try for the next episode."

"Oh, right."

She actually had a good time with Erin. The conversation started professionally as they discussed the merits of hair clips versus bobby pins before it veered into bad ex-boyfriends. It was the first time she'd participated in a deeper, personal conversation with her. Layla had listened in for two years as Erin and Suzan, the other hair and make-up artist, chatted over her about their lives but she'd never joined them. Now she found herself in the position of being able to offer advice on how Erin could protect herself from people like Jeremy Bowen who wanted to use her position. She completely skipped the part where she hadn't taken her own advice until it was too late.

Their chat ran so late that Layla darted into the meeting room just as the clock on the wall flashed over to :01. "Apologies," she said to the room as she took her seat.

The read went fine until they got to the end of the second act. Layla scanned ahead and swallowed when she saw what was about to happen to her character. She knew that she didn't have many friends in the cast but, seeing the upcoming scene, she was going to have to lower that number to none.

Two seasons of looking out for only herself had led her to this low point. She had nobody else to blame. Well, there was one other person who wasn't in the room, so this situation was on Layla. She had at least one more season, more if the show got lucky. If she was ever going to turn this around, she was going to have to take her lumps and pick herself up from the very bottom, starting now. They finished the scene and every actor at the table looked at her expectantly.

"Is there a problem?" Chris Peck, the show's lead and her television husband Zeus asked.

"The thing with the wine," Layla began.

"Jesus, Layla, it's a joke." His voice was sharp. Since Chris had found out about her involvement in the car crash that injured his new girlfriend, their already strained professional relationship had been pushed to the very edge. "It's just a glass of wine, for fuck's sake."

"It would be better if he used the bowl of ambrosia on the table." The gelatin, marshmallow and whipped cream salad would provide a much better visual than a glass of wine as the instigating act of a fight between Hera and Eros.

Sean Glenn–Eros–spat his mouthful of water across the table. "What?"

"It's a fun episode. If we're going to do this scene, we might as well go for it and let it deteriorate into an all-out food fight instead of sticking with half measures. The ambrosia would work better, don't you think?"

Chris stared at her hard. She didn't say another word.

Finally, Sean spoke. "Layla's right. It would be funnier." He looked at Chris's frown. "I think." Sean looked over at Warren Reams, the episode's director. "What do you think?"

It was the man's first time working on the show and

he was still learning the power politics behind the scenes. "I like it. We'll run with it," he agreed.

"One thing," Layla added.

"There it is." Chris's hatred practically burned her as she sat silently, not reacting to the insult.

"I know it's last minute but I'd like Sean and I to work with Russ first. If that stuff spills on the floor, it's going to be slippery. I'd rather have Sean not land on me." Sean was a foot and a half taller than her 4'11".

"What's slippery? The ambrosia?"

"Jello and whipped cream? Oh, yeah. Once you start wrestling in that stuff, knees and elbows can go flying very easily."

"How do you know that?" the god of love asked with a leer, much to the enjoyment of the other actors around the table.

"I went to college."

Sean dropped his glass entirely.

* * * *

He was improving. He hadn't stuttered or drooled while he talked to her. Russ Vukovich collapsed against the brick wall of the soundstage and scrubbed his face with the palms of his hands. Then he held them there when he realized they smelled like the lilac skin cream Layla used. He was such an idiot.

After he'd left the Navy, a friend of a friend had hired him to help out with his stunt business in Los Angeles. They quickly discovered that Russ's talents lay more in teaching actors how to fight than standing in for them. When a no-name show needed someone to do sword fights and wrestling, as the newbie, Russ drew the short straw. Fortunately, he got along with the cast members and when the show was renewed, his contract was too. He'd mostly worked with the men but the few scenes he'd done with Layla had reduced him to a babbling wreck.

He sniffed his hands again and forced them down to his side. He'd only come in to organize his equipment. Running into Layla had been an unexpected bonus. Before he could move, he heard shouting from around the corner. It was Layla's voice and she sounded pissed, which made it a regular day.

Two security guards he recognized were escorting a skinny dude out of the make-up trailer and the guy was not happy to leave. Russ looked at Todd Olson and nodded towards the trailer. The tall guard shook his head.

He was on his way back out when he saw Layla bolt from the trailer. A minute later, the show's tiny stylist left too, locking the door behind her. He was going to let it go until he saw that Erin had obviously been crying.

The bitch queen strikes again. Yes, Layla looked like a wet dream walking but, personality wise, Russ was glad he didn't know her other than by sight. She'd been utterly professional and completely emotionless in their sessions but she hadn't gone out of her way to annoy him like she had most of the other crew.

"Erin, are you okay? What happened?"

The woman stared up at him, surprise overtaking her red, puffy eyes. "Nothing."

"I know how hard it can be when actresses get," he paused, "difficult."

"No, it's fine."

"Layla may be one of the leads but that doesn't give her the right to make you cry. I can talk to Chris or Nick," Russ offered. Chris Peck and Nick Thurston had pulled him into their circle of friends after the Greek gods accidentally targeted him during one of their prank wars. Since then, the targeting had been on purpose until they learned that he was the person who'd invented payback. He was currently two up on them.

"She didn't do anything. My ex-boyfriend showed up and Layla called security for me to get rid of him. She was really nice about it too. She said she's going to put him on a watch list at the gate so he can't get back in."

Maybe there was a special effects shot coming up and they had a double on set. After all, the woman in the car had smiled at him. Now she'd been nice to Erin. It had to be a different person.

"We're still talking about Layla Andrews, aren't we? Hera, Queen of Olympus with the attitude to match?" he asked.

Erin smiled. "I know, right! She was really quiet last week. And nice so far this week."

"Maybe she's been replaced by a pod person." Although it was easier to not act on his crush when he knew she was a bitch. If she were nice, it would be a lot harder to stay away from her.

"I vote we keep this version."

Russ put his finger to his lips and looked over his shoulder in mock fear. "I won't tell if you don't." They shook hands in a silent pact.

* * * *

It had to be an imposter. Some kind of android look-alike. Because there was no way that Sean Glenn would be looking at the real Layla Andrews with anything near awe. He listened and nodded while he drank a bottle of water while Layla explained the set-up for the fight that was coming up. Sean stood quietly to the side, staring at her.

"Sean, you okay?"

"Hmm?"

Layla looked over her shoulder. "I think he's in

shock at the thought that I went to college."

"I'm fine with you going to college," Sean protested.

She transferred her gaze to Russ and he could have sworn the corners of her chocolate brown eyes crinkled at him. "Okay, I think he's in shock at the thought that I may or may not have wrestled in Jello and whipped cream in college."

Russ didn't understand why they thought him dropping his water bottle was so funny.

Sean left early since his part of the fight consisted mainly of not stepping on the small actress as they wrestled. Layla asked if Russ could stay a bit longer so she could run through everything a couple more times and he easily agreed. Aside from the Jello wrestling comment, which he tried very hard to forget whenever he had to position her, Layla had been her usual cool, professional self. When she was confident she had her moves down, she thanked him for his help and headed out. She got to the door before she turned around and came back.

"I need to apologize," she told him.

"Why? I thought the session went really well." She even cracked a smile. It had been a shockingly nice change actually.

"No. About not saying 'hi' to your friends at the volleyball tournament last weekend."

Russ really didn't want to get started about the tournament. That entire day was a disaster from start to finish when it came to the cast of Olympus. The plan was to have a cast member, one of the gods, serve as a fan's slave for the day and Chris was designated as the volunteer. When Zeus showed up at the contest winner's house that Saturday he learned that his now ex-assistant had tried to torpedo the whole event, going as far as to lie to the sweepstakes organizers about the winner's agreement and participation. Nobody had been informed he was coming.

According to Chris, when he knocked on Sydney Richardson's house that morning, she shut the door in his face. Russ smiled in spite of himself as he remembered Chris telling the story of hearing her dismiss him, saying "I'm busy" while he was tried to convince her to go along with the studio's publicity stunt.

She'd eventually agreed, at a price. She would help Chris out if he agreed to show up at a fundraiser she had running that day to raise money for a charity she'd established that helped burn victims like herself. She'd played her part but then Chris had ditched her before he could follow through on his half of the agreement. To make up for it, Sean, Nick and Layla had to substitute for him by attending Sydney's "Curse the Darkness" beach volleyball match. Russ tagged along—officially to act as security, unofficially to keep an eye on Layla.

Fortunately for everybody, Chris showed up eventually and the guys were a hit with the crowd, helping raise a lot of money for Sydney's foundation. Layla, on the other hand, refused to go anywhere near any of the burn victims who were there to cheer on the teams, including some of Russ's wounded military buddies in the crowd. It worked out for Chris and Sydney in the end; the pair had ended up dating and were still going strong. But the rest of the cast and crew who had been involved were still suffering through the new, added tension between Chris and Layla that the contest had raised.

"You don't have to say anything about that afternoon. At all. Really," Russ told her. The sooner he could forget about it, the better.

"I do. I'm truly sorry. I didn't mean to insult you or your friends. I just don't do well around burn victims," she tried to explain.

"It's fine."

"No, you have to understand. I really don't do well around them. When I was little, my dad was an insurance claims adjustor. On his last case, he was checking out an accident site and it blew up. My mom and I had to visit him in the burn ward every day for two months. It was…beyond horrible. He was in so much pain all of the time. I remember the smell and the bandages and the crying. It never fades. Ever since then I can't do the hospital thing. Or the burn patient thing. I've tried but I can't. So I'm sorry for disappointing you and upsetting your friends."

She didn't give him time to respond after that. He blinked and she was gone, the heavy security door clanking as the brace at the top eased it shut.

Definitely a pod person.

Chapter 2

What had she been thinking? She never talked about her dad. Ever. He'd been gone for twenty years and she could count the times she'd brought him up in conversation. It had to be Russ's eyes, all brown and sympathetic and surrounded by thick black eyelashes that probably felt like butterflies on a girl's skin when he kissed her. Yeah, it was definitely Russ's fault.

Layla fought the urge to stomp back to her trailer because she wasn't an eight-year-old but she allowed herself to throw some elbows to pick up momentum as she walked really fast. Fortunately, everyone else seemed to have left while she was rehearsing so there was nobody around to witness her pseudo-tantrum. Her not-stomp stopped dead when she saw a figure coming out of her trailer, not because she didn't want to get caught but because she wondered if she could turn and run before she was spotted.

"Laylay, I need to talk to you."

Apparently not. And her day had been going relatively well too. "I told you it's Layla at work. You're late, Kristin. Like, four hours late. We have a ton of stuff to do," Layla informed her assistant.

"I'm just here to tell you that I need the afternoon off," Kristin protested without looking up from her phone.

She didn't have to look up. Layla already knew they shared the same clear golden brown complexion and that they both had the same delicate high cheekbones and narrow jaw, courtesy of their mother and maternal grandmother. Layla had her father's hair, though, thick and black with a loose curl; there was nothing delicate about it. "No."

"Mom said I could."

"Does Mom know you've already taken five days off in the last three weeks?" Layla asked.

"Doesn't matter. I have plans. I'll be late tomorrow morning because Joy and I are having breakfast." Kristin wandered back to her car, a Lexus a year newer than Layla's, her thumbs flying on the tiny screen.

Layla lost the grip she had on her temper and banged her boots on the metal stairs. It was bad enough having her little half-sister around after Layla had—blackmailed was such an ugly word—encouraged Chris to hire her as his personal assistant. He'd lasted longer than she thought he would, but even he had limits and when Kristin almost cost him his chance for the lead role in an upcoming feature film, he reached them. The next morning Kristin had shown up – late – saying she was now working for Layla with their parents' blessing.

Nobody had bothered to ask her opinion, let alone blessing. Now she was picking up the tab for her sister's Rodeo Drive habit while being stuck doing all her assistant's work as well.

Layla texted to her mother. *K SAYS TAKING AFT AND 2MORROW MORNING OFF.*

SHE NEEDS A BREAK.

SHE'S ALREADY HAD 5 DAYS OFF THIS MONTH.

TALK AT SUPPER NEXT SUNDAY.

She was going to be somewhere else on that Sunday at supper time. Like Alaska. There was no way she was going to show up to hear lecture number four about how she should cut her sister another break and do her part in helping out her family since she was lucky enough to have such a successful career. Thanks to her family, she was lucky to have kept her job at all.

Layla booted up her computer. With Kristin gone, she was going to have to do it all herself and she might as well get it done at work. It's not like she'd be better off at her place. Layla had chosen a small apartment on purpose. After growing up in a house filled with three generations of family, she didn't want to rattle around a big empty condo by herself. She already kept a Filipino news channel on in the background so she could hear voices speaking Tagalog in the next room. Her family might drive her insane but she still missed the language and sounds of home. Layla lost track of time as she sorted fan emails into various folders according to the responses they required. A knock on the door interrupted her before she emptied her inbox.

She didn't shout "It's open" or "Come in" or any other welcoming phrase. Mostly because whoever it was, wasn't. That was why she kept it locked.

Her door rattled again. "Hey! Bitch!"

* * * *

"Stone. Cold. Bitch."

It was killing Chris Peck not to say more about his co-star. Russ was certain that the actor had already bitten his tongue at least once. Literally. As bad as things had been on set between the two of them for the last couple seasons, this year was shaping up to be worse. Russ – well, everyone – knew that Layla and Chris's new girlfriend Sydney had some kind of past but nobody was talking. Until this morning, Russ wouldn't have blinked at the comment.

"I'm sorry you got stuck with her, Russ," Chris continued. "I was so shocked that she suggested the change, when I agreed to it, it never occurred to me that you'd be the collateral damage. I swear that it wasn't another prank. Pranks are supposed to be funny."

"It was fine, Chris." Russ took a swig of his second 'apology' beer. "She was actually really good this afternoon."

"It was strange," Sean agreed. The red-headed former basketball player hadn't said a lot since he'd arrived at the bar. Every once in a while he'd mutter something about Jello wrestling but that was about it. "She listened to me when Russ and I were making suggestions."

Pod person, Russ thought again. It had to be. He wasn't going to complain about it although this new, nicer version of Layla was going to play hell with his sleep habits. He had a hard enough time getting to sleep when he didn't know her, pun intended. Realizing he wanted to be around her was going to make it ten times worse.

He lost track of the guys' conversation as he recalled hers. She'd apologized. She'd offered personal information. He didn't know how much of it was true but it was something. Hell, the fact that she talked to him at all. She didn't order or insult or ignore. For the first time since he'd been introduced to her, she'd acted like an actual human being. Perhaps his theory was wrong. Maybe the woman he first met was the pod person and this was the real Layla. Crap, his imagination did not need that kind of encouragement.

"Russ?" Nick elbowed his ribs. "Dude, where'd you go?"

"What?"

"I asked you how your Marine buddy was doing. Trent. From the volleyball game," Nick Thurston repeated. The actor had been subdued after meeting actual warriors a couple weeks back. They'd made an impact to the point where he'd heard that Nick was shifting his on-screen character to reflect them.

"Navy buddy. He's good. Home. He liked meeting you. All the guys did," Russ added.

Chris glowered at him and Russ realized he'd brought them back to the volleyball game and Layla's behavior on that particular afternoon. "I'm sure they would have liked to have met Layla too but she wouldn't go talk to them because she's a bitch."

"She apologized about that."

Sean sprayed his beer across the table.

"Sean, what is with you and drinks today?" Nick asked his sputtering buddy.

"Layla apologized? Layla?" Sean repeated.

"Yeah. I'm a little shocked myself."

"Layla?"

"Yes."

"Layla?"

"Sean, enough. She apologized about not meeting them."

"Did she give you some kind of explanation?" Nick asked him.

Russ scratched the back of his head. She had but he really didn't feel like sharing it with the guys. It was like a secret that he had with her. He liked the connection. If he shared her story, he wouldn't have it to himself anymore. "It's personal," he settled on.

"You've got to give us more than that," Sean begged.

"No, I don't." Russ finished his beer. "Thanks for the drinks, Chris. See you tomorrow." He wasn't worried about the booze. They were at a bar a few blocks away from the studio and Russ had left his car there. By the time he walked back, he'd be fine to drive home. It also gave traffic a little more time to clear. He loved L.A. but he would never get used to rush hour. All one-hundred-

and-eighty minutes of it.

He stopped to compare fantasy baseball teams with the security guards at the main gate so it was close to an hour before he got back to his car, which was parked at the Olympus soundstage. The tail lights of his pick-up flashed as he turned off the alarm, and the single beep sounded at the same time he thought he heard something coming from the trailers.

He hesitated and listened but heard nothing. He was reaching for the door handle when he heard a woman scream. After twenty episodes, he recognized Layla's shouts but he knew they weren't filming. Another scream echoed across the deserted parking lot.

Russ saw the footprint on the trailer door from the base of the stairs. He missed the torn metal frame until he grabbed it to swing it open but he didn't blink as its jagged edge cut into his palm. Russ took one step into the trailer and saw Layla flat on her back, bleeding from her face, while a familiar looking man bent over her, fist raised.

He was already reaching for the guy when Layla kicked out from her position on the floor. She caught her attacker in the shoulder, booting him up and back. Russ grabbed hold of his jacket and, adding to the guy's momentum, tossed him out the door and over the metal hand rail.

"Don't let him get away," Layla gasped as she pushed herself up to her elbows.

"You're bleeding!"

"Get him!"

Russ glanced out the door at the unmoving heap on the concrete. Layla's attacker had both arms trapped under his body and one leg caught in the railing. Russ pulled out his phone as he lifted Layla with one arm and sat her on the only part of the sofa that still had an intact cushion. "I need security and police to Layla Andrew's trailer immediately. She's been attacked and needs medical attention." She slapped his arm at that last line but he ignored her as he finished his conversation.

"I don't need medical attention," she said when he hung up.

"Your nose is bleeding."

Layla touched her nose, then winced. "It's not broken. Just sore." She poked at the swelling below her left eye. "But that one's going to leave a mark." She leaned around him and tried to look out the door. "Are you sure he's not getting away?"

"I'm sure." He wasn't going anywhere. "Can I ask you a question?"

"Sure."

"Why does Chris hate you so much?"

"You walk into this and that's your question? I assumed it was going to be about..." She indicated her destroyed trailer.

"Never assume. Chris. There must be a reason."

Layla pointed to the mini-fridge behind him. "There's an icepack in there. There is a reason but I can't tell you. Legally."

Russ bent his six foot frame in half to get low enough to reach into the tiny freezer. He tossed a gel pack to her and she pulled it out of the air with her left hand.

"If you can't talk about that, can you talk about the guy kissing the pavement?"

Layla eased the icepack onto her cheekbone, and collapsed bonelessly against the back of the sofa. "That is Dickhead Jeremy."

"Friend of yours?"

She glared at him with one eye. "He's Erin Thorne's

ex. He was here this morning—"

"That's who I saw!" Russ interrupted. "I thought security removed him from the property."

Layla lowered the icepack. "So did I."

There she was, the queen bitch of Olympus. This time, however, Russ thought she might be underplaying it. Security was supposed to be on the ball, especially when it came to specific complaints. Despite all the drama that surrounded Layla, he'd never heard a peep about her abusing security. If she'd filed a complaint, it should not have fallen through the cracks. The fact that it had with such visual results meant that heads were going to roll.

The rent-a-cops were full of swagger as they approached the trailer. Once they saw the body and heard the groaning, things got serious in a hurry. The older man radioed for back-up, which Russ took as they'd ignored his earlier request, and the younger man tried to roll Jeremy over but his screams stopped him. He radioed for an ambulance.

"Hey, Miss Andrews needs to be looked at first," Russ shouted over the railing.

The younger man amended his request and stood up so Russ could read his ID. "Is she alright?"

"Don't you think you should have asked that first, Wilder?" Russ could feel the level of adrenaline in his bloodstream rising by the second as shock wore off and his body chose fight over flight. The physical altercation was over but now he was pumped. Tossing that guy around wasn't enough. If Jeremy wanted to beat on somebody, he should have gone after someone his own size. Right now, Russ was up for a rematch.

"Russ, don't say any more," Layla said quietly from the sofa.

"What?"

"Don't say anything. I'll tell them he attacked me and when I kicked him off me he went out the door and over the railing."

"Layla, don't lie for me. I kinda helped him over."

"You aren't covered for this."

This asshole wasn't going to try to sue her, was he? "Do you have insurance for this?"

A pained, funny look crossed her face. "I have insurance for everything. You wouldn't believe my premiums. Besides, it will keep your name out of the papers."

Wilder and Olson called in LAPD and paramedics. The ambulance arrived first. The EMT examined Layla carefully. She assured the woman she was okay. She was a good enough actress to pull off "fine" while trying to staunch the bleeding from her nose. Russ, however, felt the need to point out she'd been knocked to the ground at least once.

He ought to have kept his mouth shut.

The cops showed up just as Layla was lifting the back of her shirt to prove to the paramedic that she was "perfectly fine." Russ saw a pair of red splotches on her back that were already deepening into purple. When the EMT hissed, he realized he'd missed something. "What?"

The woman circled her finger above the larger mark. "That's a boot print."

Layla dropped her head and sighed.

"Why didn't you say something?" Russ shouted.

"I figured 'Dickhead Jeremy beat the crap out of me' covered it!"

"We should get x-rays," the paramedic said. "We can call another bus for Ms. Andrews."

"I don't need x-rays. I'm fine," Layla insisted.

The police took her statement while Russ stood guard over the back of the sofa. His statement was briefer. He specifically told them that he was the one who'd tossed Jeremy to the ground. Nobody seemed to have a problem with it. He also stressed the fact that Layla's attacker had been removed by security once already that day and wondered aloud how he managed to get back onto the lot.

The assault charge alone was enough for the cops to hold Jeremy, last name Bowen. The two baggies of white powder in his pocket sealed the deal. After promising that he and Layla would be at the station the next morning to sign statements, Russ loaded the petite actress into his truck.

He would have preferred to take her to the hospital to be checked over but she refused. She barely made it through the paramedic's exam. For a minute he thought he'd have to sit on her, and not in a fun way. Layla looked progressively worse as the check-up went on, her skin becoming cool and clammy. The only reason he knew that was because she'd grasped his hand when the stethoscope came out and hadn't let go until the ambulance left. Her narrow fingers were white but his hand was so large under hers that she didn't have a chance at cutting off any circulation. Layla didn't even look embarrassed when she let go. That's when he knew it was serious.

Then she wouldn't let him take her to her parents' house. She'd categorically refused to call her sister to the point where she reached for the door handle when he pressed the issue. He refused to leave her alone so she'd capitulated and they agreed he'd drive her home. She hadn't spoken a word since then, not even a complaint.

Pod person.

Chapter 3

"How the hell do you have Kristin's phone number?" Layla gripped the door knob and twisted the key in the deadbolt above it so hard she thought it might sheer off. Russ had insisted not only on driving her home but also on seeing her into her apartment. On any other day, having him in her home would have been the stuff that dreams were made of. Tonight, though, her head was pounding too much to enjoy even the idea of it.

"She gave it to me."

"Of course she did." Russ was gorgeous. He wasn't a movie star like Chris and Nick but looks-wise he could be if he wanted to. He also had something darker to him that the actors lacked. Maybe it was his stint in the military. Layla's head understood that his edge had been hard earned and was not necessarily a good thing. The other parts of her stopped thinking once they realized how sexy it was.

"You don't want to go to your parents' house and you don't want me to call your sister to stay with you. Who is going to keep an eye on you tonight?"

The man was a pit bull. "I don't need anyone to keep an eye on me. I'm fine," Layla promised. She crossed her heart. Anything for him to just go away.

"What if you have a concussion?"

"It's just a headache."

"How do you know? You refused to go to the hospital. You need somebody to stay and keep an eye on you and if you won't call your family, I'll do it."

By the time they'd finished with security and the police and the EMTs it had been after midnight. Layla was out of fight. The over-the-counter pain killers Russ stopped to buy on the way to her place hadn't kicked in yet and she'd been up since way too early. "Fine. I'll make up the sofa."

He fit. Mostly. It was a six foot long sofa and he needed every inch. She settled Russ and ducked into her room as soon as humanly possible. Layla thought she'd have trouble sleeping with him in the next room but it wasn't because she was scared.

She was out of practice with a man sleeping over. In fact for the last two years she was out of practice with men in general. Except for mandatory work engagements with an actor who'd been recruited by her agent or the studio as her date, she hadn't had any presence in the social scene at all. Now that she had her life back, Layla had intended to slowly re-enter the dating world. A good guy like Russ was supposed to be the final goal, not her starting point. Of course, this wasn't the overnighter she'd been aiming for.

Layla rolled over and looked at the clock. She'd already wandered into the kitchen for some water and accidentally-on-purpose checked to see if the blanket she'd given Russ had slipped off his chest. It had and she learned that Russ had stripped down to his jeans to sleep. She felt no guilt at turning the air-conditioning up a couple degrees to make it warmer than normal since that was the result. She'd turned on the ceiling fan in her bedroom to compensate for herself.

It was almost two and sleep was no closer than it had been an hour ago. Layla drained the glass on her night table and debated whether or not she was willing to make another kitchen run. She might be awake but Russ had had a long day too. A strip of light glowed under her bedroom door. Russ had turned on the lights.

Layla eased her bedroom door open. "Are you okay?" she asked softly.

"Can't sleep," he whispered back.

Layla tightened the sash on her bathrobe and shuffled over to the overstuffed armchair by the window. The thick grey carpet absorbed the sound of her footfalls. "Want to talk about it?"

"I really don't like it when I see a woman getting beat up."

"As a woman, I thank you."

"I'm not kidding, Layla."

"I know. I also know that what happened this afternoon was not your fault. It had nothing to do with you." She sighed.

"What?"

"I'm really hoping this doesn't come back onto Erin. It wasn't her fault either and the cops are going to question her."

"It's nice that you're trying to protect her but she invited her drug-dealing ex to her workplace."

"She thought he was going to pay her back some money he owed. Just because a person's done something wrong in the past, it doesn't mean you can always assume that they're going to do worse in the future. Sometimes it's just a mistake that gets out of hand."

By the end of that little defensive argument, Layla felt a tightness in her throat that usually meant her voice had risen. She hoped it was just her but Russ noticed as well. He sat up and swung his feet to the floor.

"Are we still talking about Erin here?" he asked.

She shrugged. "I came out here for a glass of water."

"Sit."

She did. It was instinct. He used that same tone when they were about to try a tricky stunt move and not paying attention resulted in her getting her butt kicked.

"This thing you did wrong, is this the thing that

involves Sydney?"

Of course Russ had met darling Sydney. Most of the cast had and Chris's girlfriend had charmed them all. "I had an accident. I made a good decision but it ended up going wrong. It went really, really wrong but it was an accident." If you're going to drink, don't drive. That mantra had been drilled into every teenager since high school and she'd listened. It was her bad luck that the message hadn't made the same impact on other people. "Then I made a bad decision on purpose to try and fix the accident-causing one and things really went to hell."

"And now you are stuck with the on-purpose mistake?"

"If I tried to fix it again, everything would just get worse. So I'm living with the consequences."

Russ leaned forward, his knees almost touching her. "Layla, what did you do?"

"I can't say."

"I won't tell."

"I believe you." She still couldn't tell. Wouldn't tell, not when there was still a chance it might eventually work out in the end, however slight. "I want to but I can't. I promised I wouldn't and I'd really like to keep that promise. I have to live with what happened and the easiest way is to say nothing at all. Please understand."

"Okay."

"Thank you." Thank God. Why couldn't the day just end already? She'd obviously been wrong thinking it was going to be a good one. Tomorrow she'd be smarter and not expect miracles.

"One more question?

"No. The paramedics asked questions and the cops asked questions and you asked questions. I'm all questioned out." If she hadn't been so tired, she might have let him ask. The problem was that she might have answered. Russ was kind and gentle and even though his voice was still gravelly and sexy when it was soft it was really easy to listen to and obey. She couldn't afford to slip up now. The past was done. Talking about it wouldn't change anything.

"Fair enough, Layla." Russ lay back down on the sofa and pulled up the blanket. "Good night."

* * * *

Russ wasn't used to anyone beating him into the shower. The sound of running water broke into his rough sleep and he opened his eyes to find the apartment still dark. The clock on the cable converter shone a dim green 5:57 a.m. which meant on top of everything else, he'd overslept. He should be two miles in already. He could count the number of morning runs he'd missed this year on one hand. He couldn't head out now because they had to get to the police station and sign statements before Layla had to show up for rehearsal. The day was not starting out well.

Then the water in the shower turned off and Layla stuck her towel-wrapped head out of the bedroom door. "There's coffee ready on the counter. Or hot chocolate or tea if you want. Oh, and bagels. Plates are in the cupboard. The margarine is in the fridge door." At least there were bagels; he could live without cream cheese if he had to.

The first cupboard was an adventure. Packages of Pancit noodles and cracker nuts rained down on his head. He briefly noted that he'd never heard of either as he stuffed them back between cans of coconut milk and a bag of jasmine rice. He assumed that she had a housekeeper who had tossed the groceries in like that because it didn't seem like something he actress would do; Layla was always one-hundred percent put together on set. She never looked like a stuff-it-in-the-corner kind of girl. The second cupboard revealed the plates and—there was a God and he liked Russ—travel mugs.

Taking care of the statements was surprisingly easy, mostly requiring only a review and signature. They headed back to the studio in his truck since they'd left Layla's car on the lot overnight. Layla still wasn't talking but the silence was comfortable.

He watched out of the corner of his eye as Layla flipped down the sun shield and adjusted it so she could look into the mirror. She poked at the bruising around her eye. Ice had taken care of most of the swelling but even make-up couldn't hide the rainbow. "What's wrong? Do you need another pill?" he asked.

"No."

"So what's the problem?"

"Reams is going to have a fit and somehow Chris is going to make this all my fault."

He wished he could argue. "If he's there when we get there, I'll talk to him."

Layla shook her head. "It's okay, Russ. I can handle him."

"I never said you couldn't." Man, she took difficult to a whole new level. Then again, now that he thought about it, he couldn't remember a single time she'd asked him for a favor. He hadn't heard of her asking anyone else either. "You don't like asking for help, do you?"

"No."

That much about her he knew. She was not a team player. He got lucky when he enlisted. He hadn't wanted to go for the capital "T" Teams but he'd ended up with some really good guys. Russ was still looking for that kind of camaraderie outside of the service. He liked his current job and was grateful for it but it wasn't what he wanted to do for the rest of his life.

"Like I said, if he arrives before I go, I'll talk to him."

"Aren't you working today?"

Russ shook his head. "I've got an interview."

She stared at him head on. He hadn't expected to get her full attention with that comment. "Like for a magazine?"

"Like for a job."

"You're going to work on a different show? That'll suck. For me. Us. I mean you're good and we'll all miss you if you leave."

He chanced a glance at her and could see a faint blush on her dark cheeks. "You'll miss me?" he teased. "That's so sweet."

"What's the job?"

Russ winced. He hadn't meant to spill the beans that he was even looking at new employment.

"You don't have to tell me," Layla said quietly.

"Nobody else knows." He hesitated. His passenger waited patiently. When it seemed like he wasn't going to share any more, she turned her head and stared at the lines of cars crawling along the freeway. "My brother is starting a security company. I have a chance to get in on the main floor."

Layla nodded. "Business with family can be tricky. Do you think you can work together?"

"I think so. Personally, we get along fine. My parents think we might kill each other but professionally we balance each other out well."

"That sounds like a good opportunity then. You worked security and electronics when you were in the navy, right?"

"How did you know that?" He didn't think she knew anything about him beyond his name and the fact that he knew how to handle bladed weapons. It was flattering.

"I listen. I'll bet you were good at it. You handled Dickhead Jeremy without any problems. I have an easier time seeing you do that than I do seeing you teach fencing. Although you're really good at that too," she added.

Russ laughed. "You softened Bowen up for me first." She blushed again. "It's not even close to a done deal so I'd appreciate it if you don't say anything. I like working on Olympus and I have a contract till the end of the season. I wouldn't be making any decisions until then anyway."

"I won't say anything. I promise."

It was the weirdest thing. He believed her.

Chapter 4

Her second day of freedom started off even more promising than the day before had. Yesterday hadn't begun with a hot, half-naked man in her apartment. Today she even got some intelligent conversation with breakfast. Most importantly, he'd left her enough coffee to fill up her travel mug before heading out. That was the sign of a real gentleman. If the good news continued beyond arriving at work, she'd be ahead of the game.

The stop at the cop shop didn't take long at all so they were among the first to arrive at work. Layla was certain that Russ had conjured some driving voodoo when they hit the freeway. Every lane they were in was the fastest moving, and gaps magically appeared whenever he'd needed to change from one to another. She was glad to be early.

She made a bee-line over to the make-up trailer. Russ hung behind, staring at the repairs being made to her trailer. Layla noticed that the interior door screen had already been replaced and somebody was washing off the footprint on the exterior one. If Dickhead Jeremy hadn't realized that trailer doors opened out and not in, he wouldn't have given her the warning she needed to prepare herself for a fight. She raised a hand to her face and realized how lucky she'd been to have those few extra seconds.

Erin was in the make-up trailer waiting for her. Layla tolerated the hugs and arm patting and the repetitive "I'm okay but are you okay?" declarations as Erin told her about her experience giving her first police statement. Russ caught Layla at the door. "Are you two okay?"

Both women laughed at the question. "The police asked Erin a lot of questions but everything she said matched everything I said. So that's good," Layla said. She smiled at Erin again, who smiled back. She couldn't remember the last time that had happened without a camera rolling.

"Chris isn't here so I'm going to take off," Russ told her quietly while Erin answered her phone.

"Good luck," Layla whispered back. She crossed her fingers and waggled them at him.

Russ reached out and gently brushed her cheek, right at the edge of where the bruising started. "You too. If anybody gives you trouble, you let me know."

She couldn't help herself. She tilted her head and leaned into his touch. It was warm and safe. Staying there forever wouldn't be a problem. She had no idea why he was being so kind, or why he was looking out for her but it sure as hell was a nice change from going it alone. "Thank you." For more than he knew.

Maybe he did because his eyes got a little bigger before he pulled his hand away.

Layla had no idea how far he got before somebody outside the trailer started screaming for security. She looked at Erin, who was frozen in panic. "Do you think Jeremy came back?" the stylist asked.

She knew that voice. "No, I don't think that's it."

"Fired! You're fucking fired!" Kristin burst into the trailer. "My sister was attacked by your boyfriend and it's all your fault. She could have died!" Her half-sister had three inches on her thanks to Kristin's father's genes, but she was still three inches shorter than Erin. The height differential was skewed in the stylist's favor but Kristin had bitchiness on her side. "Get your stuff and get gone before I call security on you."

Fat tears rolled down Erin's cheeks. "Miss Aquino, I'm so sorry for what happened to your sister. I'll go."

"Wait a minute, you bitch," Layla snapped, stepping between the two women. She looked over her shoulder at her new friend. "Not you," she said to Erin.

There was a commotion in the doorway that she was doing her best to ignore as jostling bodies fought for position. She saw Chris fighting to step into the trailer and join in the screaming and Russ behind him, holding the star back.

"Laylay, what are you doing?" Kristin demanded. "You were attacked because of her. I'm handling the situation."

"It's Layla and leave Erin alone. I was attacked because Dickhead Jeremy is an idiot." Layla knew she should stop talking but everything she'd wanted to say for months was coming out of her mouth and her internal mute button was nowhere to be found. "First of all, I'm fine. Secondly, Erin is not to blame. Thirdly, the cops and security are handling the situation. Finally, you were partially right. Somebody is going to be losing her job." She didn't turn her head at the sharp intake of breath by Erin behind her. "But it's going to be you. I'll have any personal items sent to the house. Right now, get out of here."

Her sister went silent. For a nanosecond. "You're firing me?"

"Yup." And it felt good. Layla hadn't wanted to have her flighty little sister around in the first place, especially as an unofficial babysitter sanctioned by her parents. "You've caused more problems than I want to think of when you were working for Chris and you've almost gotten me fired twice. On the rare occasions when you are here, you sure as hell aren't working. I'm not even going to get into that stunt you pulled on Sydney where you disappeared and left me hanging out to dry when it went bad on you."

"As soon as the name 'Sydney Richardson' came up as the contest winner, I knew I had to do something to protect you. I knew she was going to cause problems so I tried to cut her off at the pass by forcing them to take the runner up. When that didn't work, I came up with the toga plan. When I suggested it to Martine as your idea, I figured Sydney would cut and run rather than show-off her scars. I couldn't have known she'd stick around like she did. It's not my fault that Chris's new girlfriend didn't get the hint she should leave after that. Everything I did was to help you."

"Help me?" Layla's voice cracked in disbelief. "On what planet was that helping?"

A male voice growled from the door. "That was you, Kristin? I can't believe that I'm agreeing with Layla but she's right. Your ass is so fired."

That was nice. When Sydney had arrived on set for the contest's public relations photo shoot, she'd been offered the chance to wear the official costume of Olympus. At the time, only Layla and Kristin knew about the burn scars covering the woman's shoulder and back. Sydney had freaked out at the suggestion and Chris had blamed Layla for the implied insult to his guest. Layla had claimed innocence but he hadn't believed her, until now. "I don't need your kind of help, Kristin. In fact, I think it is more than past time for you to explore new employment opportunities that don't involve bleeding your sister dry."

Fortunately, the security that her sister had originally screamed for arrived. It felt liberating to see a cursing Kristin be led away even if Layla knew she'd pay for it later. It would be one more reason for her family to be disappointed in her. She tried not to think about it since, as far as they were concerned, the list was ever growing.

She took a breath and dared to turn around and look at Erin. The stylist stared at her without saying a word. "Are we okay?" Layla asked. Erin flew at her and wrapped her arms around her shoulders. "Again with the hugging," she sighed, prompting the other woman to let her go with a giggle. Russ smiled and waved goodbye from the door. She caught his eye and mouthed the word "luck." He shot her a thumbs-up and disappeared, leaving her staring at her biggest enemy on set.

Chris Peck's perpetual frown faltered for a minute before he too vanished.

It was progress.

* * * *

A person could never go wrong when going retro. This was really retro. The office was straight out of a 1930's detective movie. Leather chairs that were comfy but not overstuffed. A square cut crystal decanter full of amber liquid with matching glasses on the sofa table between the two windows that overlooked the street below. He even recognized the antique photo of the Big Apple that used to be in the bedroom beside his growing up. The only anachronism was the monitor sitting on his potential boss's solid oak desk.

The digs were surprisingly posh for the money that Leo had saved. Russ knew his brother was aiming for mid-to upper-class clientele but the set-up was extremely nice. He began to wonder if Leo had shot his wad on the décor and that's why he was looking for investors now. Layla had a point when she said working for family could be tricky. As soon as he'd heard that Leo put in for retirement after twenty years with the LAPD, Russ had known that his brother would be unable to make the switch into the corporate world and that self-employment would be his best bet. He hadn't been surprised when Leo announced his new venture.

Russ stretched out his six-foot frame on the chair angled towards the door. Leo didn't have a problem with authority so much as he had a problem with stupid. He had no tolerance for it. As a cop, Leo had been forced to deal with people who pissed him off on a regular basis because it was part of the job. Russ had no idea how his brother thought he'd be able to handle irritating clients since they were the ones with the money. Although, bringing Russ on was a good business move since this was a weakness that he could cover. The actors and actresses on Olympus weren't stupid but they stretched his patience to the breaking point on a weekly basis. He was willing to bet that his ability to deal with the general public was better than anyone else Leo was willing to work with. It was a marketable trait he knew the man wanted.

"What's the deal, Leo?" The upside of working with family was knowing exactly when the other party was throwing bullshit your way.

"What? No pleasantries? Mom would be upset," the taller, darker, older lookalike mocked.

"Leo."

"Fine." Leo pulled a file from the top drawer of the credenza behind him. The framed family photos on top rocked as the drawer slammed shut. Leo steadied the multi-generational picture with their African-American grandmother and Russian grandfather in the center of a brood of their children and grand-children. He slid it across the wide desk.

Russ listened as he flipped the pages of the contract. The buy-in was for forty thousand dollars, which would drain all of his savings. As a partner, he wouldn't be eligible for a salary either; it was all profit sharing. But the projections looked damn good.

"Where are you getting these numbers?" Russ demanded.

"From Tom. Keep reading."

He did. He knew Leo was a good salesman but it seemed a little too good. Until he got to the third partner. "Holy shit, you brought Marcus Bolling into this? The guy is an electronics wizard." He was also a complete horn dog if a woman was within fifty yards but a top-notch guy in his field. The Texan's reputation was a tremendous asset that they couldn't put a number on.

"What do you say, Russ? Your skills are being wasted teaching these people how to pull a punch. You could be making a difference to people's lives here. You could be saving lives instead of making pretend," Leo pressed, going for the hard sell and appealing to the oaths they'd both taken.

Before Russ could react, his phone rang. "Sorry, I thought I'd turned it off."

Leo waved off his apology. "Do you need to take it?"

He checked the number. Studio security was finally returning his call. "Yeah, do you mind?"

Leo tried to give him privacy as he accepted the call but his brother dropped any pretense at eavesdropping as Russ lost it on the guy at the other end of the call.

Russ couldn't believe it. Apparently, no reports had been filed after Layla's first run-in with Jeremy Bowen. The two guards on scene hadn't said a word about removing the dealer or barring him from re-entering the lot. Bashir, the guy in charge, was trying to push it back on the unpopular actress.

"No," he insisted. "Miss Andrews didn't neglect to inform your men of the situation. Your men neglected to get off their asses and file the damned reports. Because they were laying down on the job, Jeremy Bowen beat the living hell out of a four-foot-eleven actress and nearly broke three of her ribs. So don't tell me 'no harm, no foul', Bashir, because you're not going to be able to cover your ass on this one. I'll be back there in an hour with copies of the police report and I expect you to act on them appropriately." Russ let him rant for a minute and then cut him off again. "You think I'm an asshole? I could step away but then you'd be dealing with Miss Andrews and her lawyers. What's it going to be?" He didn't like to use Layla's reputation but sometimes it did serve a purpose. "Excellent. I'll see you then."

Leo was smiling at him when he ended the call. "I didn't realize you were already working a protection detail."

"Fuck off. I'm not. One of the actresses was attacked last night and security is trying to blame the victim."

His friend nodded. "Layla Andrews. You've mentioned over family dinners that she's quite the handful."

"I thought she was stuck up but we've been talking lately. I think she's just really cautious about letting people get close to her. Besides, the asshole in question had been hassling somebody else earlier in the day and Layla had him removed. That should have been the end of it. Now security is saying she lied about Layla calling him but I saw her show the call log on her phone to the officers on the scene. She doesn't have anybody else to watch her back so I'm doing it."

"I knew you'd be good at this job."

"I have a good thing going right now. Good people," Russ hedged.

Leo, the bastard, knew what he was doing. "I'm not

asking for your firstborn, Russ. With my luck, he'd be a bigger pain in the ass than you. Just think about it. I know you're still under contract to that show of yours for now and you'll want to see this Layla Andrews thing through to the end because that's what you do. I have a fourth partner lined up, a buddy out of Seattle, but I'll need an answer from you soon."

There went his wiggle room. Russ had already put Leo off for two weeks. Related or not, it was a business and Russ owed him that much. "I'll let you know by the end of the month," he promised.

Russ turned the engine over and sat in the cab of his truck with the window open, trying to catch his breath. He had to make a decision now. No, that wasn't quite right. If he were honest with himself, he'd made the decision a week ago. The problem was that the cost had just escalated and he wasn't sure if he was willing to pay the price.

Chapter 5

It had been a decidedly normal week and, for Layla, that made it extraordinary. She'd had a regular work week where she worked with her costars like a regular person. It was fabulous. There was still a definite chill in the air whenever she was around but it was now a mild frost rather than a deep freeze. Layla figured that part of it had to be sympathy after the attack although it helped that everybody knew she wasn't holding Erin responsible for it. Her firing of Kristin had also gained her some goodwill. The director had even found a way to work around her injuries. He arranged to film the post-food fight shots first with the intention of giving "Hera" a black eye during the stunt itself. His idea worked in more ways than one because when the time came, she and Sean fought dirty.

Layla knew she was going above and beyond in her attempt to make up ground and that she was using Sean to do it. He realized it as well but he wasn't complaining. Her food-fight partner was an actor by chance, not by choice, and his popularity balanced out his lack of skill for the most part. But he needed help with his acting and he knew it. In between practice sessions with Russ, she taught him a couple minor tricks of the trade that he was able to immediately put into practice. She grinned to herself when the others noticed the improvement in his ability to hit his mark for the cameras without glancing at the floor but kept her mouth shut. Yes, she was buying something close to friendship but she had to start somewhere.

Unlike standard Greek mythology where Eros helped Hera out on occasion, the show had created an antagonistic relationship between the gods on the show.

Sean looked at her hesitantly as they took their places and he saw the bowls of ammunition on the table. Layla shook her head at him. "Don't worry. Just do it. All you have to do is follow the script."

Then the director called "action." After the first take, the togas were trashed but the fight was legendary. At least half the gag reel was going to come from this episode. Four years of college basketball had Sean landing glops of ambrosia on her from across the table without a single missed shot. The marshmallows and whipped cream were squishy but it was the gelatin that stained the white linen of her toga like a bitch. She and Sean had gone at it hard and did some serious cosmetic damage to each other but the sessions with Russ had paid off. Layla's face hurt from smiling as she trooped back to shower and change while some hapless production assistants tried to clean and restage the set.

Erin was waiting for her in the trailer. "I wanted to watch but I couldn't get away. How'd it go?"

Layla had kept her new friend up to date with her rehearsals. She had the feeling that Erin was helping to smooth the way among the other actors and Layla was grateful her up-beat reports were being passed on. "Awesome. Sean nailed it. Fingers crossed that we'll only need one more take. I don't know if we have enough costume changes for more than that."

Erin sprayed something that shellacked Layla's hair flat against her skull and made sure all errant locks were tucked back into her braids. "What's it like?" Erin asked.

"What?"

"The ambrosia."

She couldn't contain the shiver that rolled down her spine. "Oh my god, that stuff is so disgusting. You wouldn't think it would be but it's insanely slimy.

Stepping in it is gross beyond words." They might be editing out her squeals in post but her costar was the one who'd cut lose with a couple of vulgarities that wouldn't be heard again for two and a half millennia.

Erin stepped away while the make-up artist powdered the bruise around her eye. It had faded a lot over the week but wasn't quite gone yet.

The stylist spun her chair and gave her another shot of hairspray from the back. "Are you ready to go again?"

"Absolutely."

"Good, cause we're ready for you," a male voice said from the door.

Twenty episodes in the can and not once had Chris Peck escorted her to the set. The actor voted one of the sexiest men on television didn't say anything as they walked back. Reams was calling for places when Chris said, "Sean said this wasn't as much fun as it looked. But it's looking great."

Holy crap, it was almost a compliment. Scratch that, it was a compliment. From the king of the gods himself. "Thanks," she managed to reply before he disappeared.

She caught a glimpse of Russ at the back of the room. He gave her a thumbs-up and she replied with a wink as she took her position.

* * * *

Every crew member Russ had ever met was watching the ultimate food fight go down. Word spread fast after the first take and now everyone wanted to bear witness. He watched Benny Duarte, the PR intern/photographer who had started a couple of weeks ago elbow gawkers out if his way in order to get shots of the about-to-be destroyed area.

"Ready on the set!" a male voice yelled, and the hubbub and shifting ceased.

Russ damned near tripped on the cables snaking over the floor when the star of his night-time dreams winked at him. Russ tugged at the waistband of his khakis, trying to magically expand them to give him some more room. It didn't work so he stood still in the shadows, watching Layla do her thing and waiting for his problem to fade away.

The dollop of whip cream that landed on her collarbone and slowly slid down the curve of her breast into the V of her toga did nothing to help his situation. Nothing at all. Fortunately by the time the director wrapped for the episode he was able to catch Layla at the door.

"Got a second?" he asked.

"For you? Sure," the queen of the gods replied.

His problem came back.

"Just let me get showered and changed. My trailer, thirty minutes?"

"Sounds good." God knew he needed the time to settle his pants again.

Russ had offered to run point on the whole Jeremy Bowen situation for several reasons, the least of which being his paranoia that Layla was right and the dude was going to sue him for assault. It turned out Russ was half right. There was talk of a lawsuit but Russ's friends on the force had let him know the dude was making noise about tagging Layla despite their statements and the photographs of her battered body. It would be a nuisance suit if it amounted to anything but it burned his ass that she was going to have to deal with it at all.

Russ wandered over to Sean's trailer to waste some time by giving him shit about causing a food fight at the office. The redheaded actor hovered over Russ and accepted the trash talk for what it was and then asked

Russ if he wanted a snack. The giant little shit tossed a Jello cup at him. Russ threw it back as he made his escape. Then he gave a nod to Sydney who was trying to sneak in to see Chris without catching any attention. She could hold her own among Chris's costars when it was absolutely necessary but she was still less than comfortable in the spotlight. He wasted another five minutes taking a slow stroll around the building until he found himself on the steps in front of Layla's door.

"Come on in," she shouted in response to his knock.

The screen door caught before the latch finally clicked home. The maintenance crew had done a good job of repairing the door but there was a bend to the frame that was going to be there until the door was replaced entirely. Some damaged things couldn't be fixed.

"Grab yourself something out of the fridge."

Over the past week, this had almost become a habit. He'd stop by to offer an update and she'd offer him a drink. "I've got news on Dickhead Jeremy," he yelled back towards the room at the end of the trailer.

Layla appeared in her everyday clothes, wrapping an elastic around the plait of her waist-length black hair. Russ watched silently as a drop of water grew at the tip of the end curl, quivered, and then splashed on the linoleum floor. He blinked when he realized she was waiting for an answer. "I'm sorry, what?"

"What's your news?"

"Good news is he hasn't gone ahead with that lawsuit he was threatening you with," he was pleased to report.

The actress slumped into the sofa's center cushion, her chin dropping to her chest. "Thank you. Good news doesn't start to cover it." Then her head came back up.

"That means there's bad news, doesn't it?"

"He made bail."

The fear that flashed in Layla's eyes made him want to squeeze the can he held into a ping pong ball but she blinked it away a second later and that cold, emotionless look he couldn't stand appeared on her face. "Do we know who posted it?"

"Nope."

Fuck, he hated that look. "What are you doing now?" They'd wrapped for the week and didn't have to be back on until Monday to start on episode three.

Layla pressed her lips together. "Trying very hard not to start cursing because I don't know if I'll be able to stop." She pulled a long draw of air through her nose and held her breath for what had to be at least a ten-count.

That did it. "Grab your coat. I'm taking you to dinner." His heart stopped beating at his show of bravado. Not even in his dreams had Layla ever agreed to go out with him. She was famous and he was...not. Russ had no idea what alien parasite had taken over his brain and made him utter those words.

"Okay."

But he was going to take that parasite and kiss it full on the lips.

Chapter 6

She was in jeans and a blouse. Jeans. She hadn't been on a date in two years and now she was dressed like she was ready for a big night out at Chuck E. Cheese. She wasn't even wearing more than minimal make-up after all the crud she'd had on her face all day. Russ wouldn't let her go change into something dressier. He said she was perfect. The man was an idiot.

He was also sneaky. When she asked "Perfect for what?" he wouldn't tell. "Trust me," he said. So she did. It was easier than she expected, trusting him. She was just as out of practice at that as she was at dating. Besides, it was only dinner. It wasn't like he could orchestrate some kind of major betrayal after a week at arm's length. He hadn't gotten nearly close enough to do that and if he were going to he would have sold the Jeremy Bowen escapade to the papers. Tonight would be fine.

They ended up at a hole-in-the-wall Mexican place miles from any landmark she recognized. The restaurant was a stand-alone building beside a community center and across from a strip mall. The entire neighborhood screamed "suburbia". Layla was afraid that if she rolled down the windows, she'd hear banjos. There was a reason she lived in Marina del Ray.

Russ had the truck in park before he turned to her and asked, "Do you like Mexican?"

"It's my favorite." It was only a little lie. She liked spicy of any flavor and Mexican was in her top five. "How did you find this place?"

Russ was at the passenger door before she was out of her seat. "It's one of those family restaurants that has been around forever but you need somebody to show it to you. You'll love it. They have a pico de gallo that will knock your socks off."

They got a couple looks from the hostess but once they were seated in a booth and were hidden from view, Layla started to relax. The waitress asked if they wanted to start with a drink and all of her nerves came back. She sat straight up in her seat, smiling blankly as she scrambled for an answer.

"Can you give us another minute?" Russ asked the girl.

Layla unwrapped the paper napkin from around the silverware and pulled off a long narrow strip. Then she did it again. When she looked up, Russ was watching her.

"Are you an alcoholic?" he asked directly.

"No. I drink. Not when I'm out though."

"Would you mind if I had a drink with supper? Or are you concerned with me driving?"

She bit her lip. It sounded like a completely reasonable request. "I know somebody who was hit by a drunk driver. It was bad. Almost fatal."

He was staring at her now. She couldn't look away. "One beer will be completely out of my system in two hours. But if it makes you uncomfortable, I won't."

Tell him it's okay. "One beer?" She'd driven after having a single glass of wine herself. He was right. One was fine, legally. With his size, he could probably have a couple and still be under the legal limit. The fact that he thought they'd still be on their date in two hours was a good sign. Get over it already.

"I don't think so. I'll have something else." He tucked the laminated bar menu behind the salt and pepper shakers against the wall.

"Order the beer. You're a grown man and I trust your judgment." She didn't want to guilt him into anything, not when he'd been so nice over the last week. This was her hang-up, not his.

"No, you don't. Not yet. But you will." Russ waved the waitress back over and ordered himself a ginger ale. Layla did the same. Then she dove into the pico de gallo with a chip in order to avoid future conversation. The gambit worked only until the dip hit her tongue. "Oh my God," she exclaimed as she hid her full mouth behind her hand, "this is fabulous!"

Russ managed to scoop half the bowl onto his chip. "I told you so. Wait until you try the enchiladas." He grinned in approval when she took his suggestion. "Those are my dad's favorite. Shit, sorry."

"What? Should I change my order?" Dammit, she liked enchiladas. If she were going to blow her diet on restaurant food, she was going to get cream sauce out of the deal.

"No, sorry for mentioning my dad," Russ clarified.

"Why would you be sorry about that? Don't you like him?"

Her date choked on his drink. Layla didn't understand why. It was a perfectly legitimate question.

"My dad and I get along fine. I didn't mean to mention it since you got so upset when you told me your father passed away in the hospital."

He looked so horrified at having started the conversation that Layla felt badly for him. "Thank God you're not an actor. You're too honest. Seriously, it's very considerate of you but that was a long time ago."

"How long?"

"I was eight."

"So, Kristin is…?"

"My half-sister. My mom remarried when I was nine."

"So Andrews isn't an Anglicized version of

Aquino?"

Layla shook her head. "My dad was from a very traditional Filipino family. The name on my birth certificate is Laylay Andrada. When my mom remarried, my dad's family was insistent that I keep his name. So everybody else is Aquino. Then I started acting and changed both to something more mainstream."

When the waitress returned, Russ was still sitting in silence, an embarrassed frown on his face. Layla asked for the enchiladas and discretely kicked him in the shins under the table to prompt him to say something to the girl. He gave his order and then apologized again when the server left with their orders. "Layla, I didn't mean to push. I'm just interested. I didn't mean to make you sad by bringing up your dad."

"It's okay. It was a sucky thing that happened when I was a kid. Your concern is appreciated but it's not necessary. Truly." She looked up to show him that she was honestly good with it and took her eyes off the prize. A glop of salsa dropped off the chip and landed on the inside of her arm. She stared at the useless remains of her napkin and tried to decide if the better bet was to use the raggedy strips or to lick off the onion and tomato juice directly.

Ever the gentleman, Russ stretched a long arm across the aisle to the next table and lifted another cutlery set. He unwrapped it and handed the fresh napkin to her before she could blink.

"Thanks," Layla said. "Are we okay now?"

"Sure?"

"Great. Let's pick a new topic of conversation. How'd the interview go?"

Apparently that was another touchy subject. At least, that's the impression she got when he started shoveling chips into his mouth and calling for another bowl of pico de gallo instead of answering her question.

"Or how about those Oakland Raiders?" she tried again.

"It's March. The season ended two months ago."

That was better. At least he was talking now. "Like I'd know. Football – that's the one with the brown ball that bounces funny when you dribble it, right?"

Russ choked. "Are you trying to commit suicide? This place is a pigskin stronghold." He pointed to three flat-screen televisions that were bolted to various walls. "Come Saturday and Sunday in the fall, this place is all football all the time."

Safe ground. "Who are the teams of choice?"

The answer led to further football questions which gave her more information on the sport than she'd ever suffered through in her life. It was fun in a weird kind of way. Date-like. If this were a date. She still wasn't sure why Russ had asked her to dinner in the first place. Layla knew she should ask but in the dark parts of her heart she wasn't sure if she wanted the answer. Pretending he was interested in her romantically was so much preferable to knowing the truth for certain.

The enchiladas were everything he promised and more. Afterwards, she enjoyed a strong black coffee while Russ enjoyed a plate of churros and chocolate sauce. He offered her some but Layla refused. It was too sweet. Unfortunately, another temptation was too much for her control on her curiosity. "Russ, can I ask you a question?"

"Sure, but can I go first?"

"Okay."

"I've been putting the pieces together with what you said before and I think I figured it out. You and alcohol and Sydney were all involved in the same accident, weren't you?"

She was out of there. Layla scooted across the seat but Russ' big work boot on the bench blocked her escape. "I told you I can't talk about that. Let me go."

"She is the person you know who got hurt, isn't she?"

Forget subtle. Occasionally being tiny had its advantages. She pulled her legs up onto the bench and hopped over her date's outstretched foot. Then she got lucky and Russ got caught behind a busboy. Layla slipped her emergency hundred-dollar bill out of her wallet and pressed it into the waitress's hand before she slipped out the front door and disappeared.

* * * *

Fuck, fuck, FUCK! He had to open his fucking mouth.

Russ had finally gotten a peek at the woman behind the mask and instead of being grateful that Layla trusted him enough to let him in at all, he'd pushed too far. Way too far. She'd told him that she couldn't and wouldn't talk about whatever the story was between her and Sydney Richardson but he wouldn't let it go. So she'd let him go.

She was fast too. For a little bit of a thing, she sure could move. It was his own bad luck that there were both a subway entrance and a bus stop across the street. She was long gone before he made it out of the restaurant. Russ didn't even know if the final straw was an insult or not but she'd paid the waitress for both their meals and left a substantial tip. He'd invited her out; the bill was his. It sat like a rock in his stomach that in the heat of the moment Layla made sure not to dine and dash. She had a real phobia about ending up in the gossip column.

It had taken some time to realize it but as much as Layla was reviled on the set, she was surprisingly out of the public eye. Yeah, reports came out from some of the cast and actors but Martine Peeples, their main PR person, kept a pretty tight leash on them. Aside from the fan contest fiasco which she couldn't get out of, she was quite invisible. She must do something to keep up with her commitments but he had no idea what projects she worked on.

Russ slowly rolled through the studio parking lot. Her Lexus was still in its spot. He figured she'd head straight home but on public transit in Los Angeles it was going to take her a while. He thought she might have detoured here. She hadn't. Now he was going to have to try to talk his way into her apartment to apologize there. That would be fun.

He should have kept his mouth shut. Not only at the restaurant but earlier in her trailer. What had he been thinking, asking her on a date? Forget about different worlds, they were galaxies apart. Layla was galas and awards ceremonies and blinding glamour and he had an old dress uniform in the back of his closet. Russ knew she was truly grateful when he kept her up-to-date about Jeremy Bowen but who wouldn't want to know where their attacker was? Anything beyond that had been all in his head. She'd only said yes to be polite.

But she'd talked to him about her father. Some people spoke about their families all the time. Layla never mentioned hers. Everybody knew that Kristin had a different last name but Russ had worked under the assumption that Layla had simply Anglicized hers. He'd put money on the fact that nobody knew they were step-sisters. Layla never mentioned the distinction.

Then there was her father. Hospitals were scary

enough for kids. Russ didn't want to think about how traumatizing it would have been to go day after day to see his own father wasting away. Between losing her dad and a sister like Kristin, no wonder Layla kept her mouth shut.

The security guard in Layla's building didn't let him up to her apartment which was a good thing considering the threats she'd had against her recently. Fortunately, he recognized Russ as a previous guest and let him know that Layla hadn't come home for the night yet.

Crap. She was out there somewhere. He could go back to the studio and see if he'd beat her to her car. Or he could stake out her apartment. The choice between stalker and creeper wasn't one he wanted to make. What he wanted was the beer he didn't have with dinner that caused this whole fucking mess.

Wait. Leo had beer.

Chapter 7

There had to be a way to recall a text message. Layla knew it could be done with emails so there had to be something she could do besides pray that somewhere out there in the night a woman accidentally dropped her smart phone into a toilet. She checked her Sent file again. Yep, it was still there. *MEN ARE IDITOS!* Sent to an unsuspecting Erin Thorne at merlot-thirty-seven. The typo wasn't the most annoying thing, although it didn't help. It was that suddenly she felt the need to share.

Her phone binged. YES THEY ARE. U OK?

Layla eyed the empty wineglass on the coffee table. Then the slightly-more-than-half-full bottle on the counter. *FINE, SORRY TO BOTHER YOU.*

NO BOTHER. DATELESS. WHICH IDIOT?

She knew that Erin didn't gossip. Actually, that wasn't true. Layla knew that the stylist didn't gossip about the other actors in the cast around her. She had no idea if Erin's discretion ran both ways. *DOESN'T MATTER. WINE TALKING. GOOD NIGHT.*

I LIKE WINE. ANY LEFT?

Layla was twenty-nine years old and didn't have a single close friend to show for it. She was tired of being alone. Since she literally couldn't end up more alone, she made her decision. *2/3 BOTTLE OF MERLOT WANT A GLASS?*

SURE. WHERE ARE U?

Layla took a breath and texted her address.

30 MINUTES. SAVE SOME WINE 4 ME.

For company, she'd open a whole new bottle.

Layla wiped down the bathroom with a towel and tossed it into the hamper, then threw all the bills and books and assorted clutter from the living room and kitchen onto the bed in her spare room and pulled the door closed. She took her hand off the wine glass in the cupboard and left it on the shelf. It would be too hard to put it back when—if—Erin was a no-show. Right now she could pretend she simply did a half-assed job tidying her apartment. If she took the glass out, she risked facing the reality of being stood up by a friend. She didn't know if she could handle that on top of an already horrendous night.

But miracle of miracles, the doorman buzzed up to clear her guest. Erin made good time. Layla bounced the crystal bowl of the goblet against the cupboard frame but managed to set it onto the counter without breaking it.

The bubbly blonde in her high heeled cowboy boots looked down on her from the doorway. "Some moron nearly fed me his tailpipe on Santa Monica and then rolled down his window to tell me I had nice tits. Tell me you didn't finish the wine," Erin begged before she even had her jacket off.

Layla couldn't help herself. She laughed and pointed at the bottle she'd moved into the living room. "I'm past the half-full mark but I put another bottle in the fridge." Without the wine, Layla would be calling herself pathetic for being so excited about having a friend over.

"So, which idiot are we drinking to? Mine or yours?" Erin snuggled into a corner of the sofa, one that had a decent view of the city skyline. The twinkling lights weren't all in the sky but it was still pretty.

It took a moment for her comment to process but when it did, it sobered Layla up quickly. "Is Dickhead Jeremy causing problems? You know he's out on bail."

"Oh, I know." Erin set down her wine glass. "You know I'm not the one who posted bail, right?"

"I didn't know who did it," Layla admitted. "I hoped

you hadn't changed your mind."

"I haven't," Erin assured her. "We are D-O-N-E. He called, to try to get back together, he said. Apparently he doesn't blame me for his arrest."

Layla bit down on her tongue so hard she thought she might have drawn blood. She so wanted to comment "Of course not, he blames me" but she didn't want to heap any more guilt on her friend. Then she thought of something more important. "You should contact the police. Or at least," she took a breath, "tell Russ."

"So we're talking about your idiot now?"

"He's not my idiot," Layla protested.

"Well he hasn't been in my trailer every day for the last week," Erin countered.

"He's been keeping me up-to-date on the Jeremy situation," Layla insisted.

"Me, too, but I've been getting texts, not in-person reports. What gives?"

Layla checked her glass. Nope, she didn't have enough wine for this conversation. Once her glass was topped up, she was ready to get into it. "He asked me out to supper."

"Finally. It took him long enough."

"What?"

"He likes you," Erin sing-songed at her.

"He does not." Oh, God, she was back in high school!

"Layla, he's been walking into walls whenever you're around since the first day he met you. You just haven't been in any frame of mind to notice."

"He has not."

"Lay-la's got a boy-friend," the sing-song continued.

"I don't!"

"Is this where the idiot part comes into play? What

did he do?"

"It was fine. Good even. But he kept coming back to this one subject I didn't want to discuss." She watched Erin's eyebrows rise in interest. "Don't ask."

"Okay. So, Russ is a big ol' dog with a bone. And?"

"He wouldn't let it go."

"So?"

"I left."

"The restaurant?"

"Yes."

"I thought he drove."

"He did," Layla said. "A bus was pulling up across the street so I jumped on and ducked so Russ wouldn't see me through the window. Then I got off at the first place I could call a taxi. It was a very nice eighty-dollar cab ride home."

Erin set down her glass. "You just ran out of the restaurant?"

"It was a brisk walk. And I paid the waitress on the way out. There's no reason she should suffer because I was having a bad date."

The stylist crushed her face into her hands. "Layla," she moaned.

"What?" It seemed like a reasonable response in the restaurant. Three glasses of wine later, not so much – but she'd been sober at the time. "What was I supposed to do? There was one subject not on the table. He didn't want to talk about his…thing and I didn't push. Was I wrong?"

"His thing or his thing?" Erin giggled.

"We didn't have time to get to his thing." If they'd had a chance to discuss Russ' thing, Erin never would have been invited over in the first place and Layla wouldn't have come up for air for days. His thing. How high school. This was great. Layla snickered to herself. Merlot always loosened her up. She must have spilled some because her glass was half-empty again already. "But what do I do now?" she asked.

"Do you want to see him again?"

"Not if he's going to keep bringing it up."

"So the next time you see him, tell him that. Exactly. Say 'I want to see you again but that subject is off limits.' The guy doesn't seem to be a complete idiot. He'll get it."

"Do you think so?"

"Of course. Talk to him on Monday. You'll see."

* * * *

"Let it go, bro. You blew it."

Russ nodded into his beer. That had been his thinking too. Goddammit he should have let it go. Layla had asked him to, had practically begged him to. He should have listened.

His cold beer bottle clinked against the two empties as he set it on the floor beside his easy chair in Leo's living room. As the oldest child of four, Leo was the first child out of the house and his first furniture purchase once he owned his own place was a big, cushy recliner just like their dad had. Russ had been the last kid out and he had to admit Leo's choice was a better one than he had made; Russ had gone for a home gym. The recliner went much better with beer.

Heading to his big brother's house had been a good idea. "I blew it big time."

"I thought you didn't like her. I didn't think anybody liked her from the stories you told."

Russ knew that Leo was sober. His brother liked to laugh at him on the rare occasions when he drank. This was the first time since high school that it was over a woman. Russ usually moved on to the next one without looking back. "I didn't know her then. She's shy. She's not bad."

"She's just drawn that way?"

"Hells, yeah." Her head didn't even come up to his shoulder unless she was wearing dangerously high heels. He'd seen her in them. That was when his drooling problem started. But even when she was in regular boots she tucked up nicely against him. He'd noticed in the elevator when he walked her to her apartment. Layla had been so tired she hadn't notice that he'd put his arm around her and led her to her door. Or maybe she had noticed and hadn't said anything because she liked it.

She wouldn't like it now. Because he was a moron. He didn't need to ask. He knew what the answer was. He didn't know the details but the link between Layla and Chris' girlfriend intersected at an accident site. The strange part was the drinking and driving piece. Russ believed her when she said she'd never done it but there had to be more to it than that. Chris wouldn't tell and Russ didn't know Sydney well enough to ask. He should let it go but he wanted to know. He wanted to know everything about the woman who'd given him a glimpse of the real her and then hidden herself away again.

"I'm never going to be able to face her again," Russ groaned.

"You could quit and come work for me. Save yourself some trouble."

"I'm giving it serious consideration."

Leo huffed. "You've been saying that for a month."

"I mean it this time."

"That's the beer talking."

"I don't think so," Russ insisted. "Our contract is up at the end of the season. Now that Olympus is so big, everybody is scrambling for it. We aren't a lock anymore."

"They like you. It'll be fine."

"I'm due for a change."

Leo hunched forward. "Are you saying I should start on the paperwork?"

Was that what he was saying? Russ fought through the beer haze. This latest disaster with Layla aside, he was near the point of moving on from the show anyway. The shine had worn off the job and it wasn't the challenge he needed. It wasn't supposed to be permanent in the first place. Having an excuse to avoid Layla was icing on the cake, especially if it really was over with her before it began.

"What if I promised to not ask her again?" Russ speculated.

"First of all, you'd ask. I know you. Secondly, no. Just no."

"Then what do I do?"

"You go back to ignoring her and staying the hell away so you can pretend it never happened. No more dinners. No more dropping by with updates. Keep it strictly business. You don't need that kind of trouble."

"Yeah." Russ finished his beer and slipped the chair into a full recline. "Yeah." He closed his eyes. As usual, big brother was right and Russ was going to follow his advice. He didn't need that kind of trouble.

He sure wanted it though.

Chapter 8

Erin was sneaky. Layla finished the bottle of merlot and Erin nursed her first and only glass for three whole sips despite the fact she'd stayed for hours. The stylist had come over to be a friend, nothing more. How cool was that? She and Layla talked and drank and laughed and talked some more. It had been awesome, even if Erin had been out to get her snookered.

Layla was a little impressed with herself. Even half in the bag, she'd given good career advice. Erin mentioned that she had an interview for a make-up opportunity over hiatus. Since they didn't know if Olympus would be picked up for another season, the cast and crew were planning their employment futures accordingly. The downtime after they wrapped for the season was a nice breather to recover from the crazy hours they put in during filming. Unfortunately whether they were renewed or not, the break was without pay; the work may stop but the bills didn't. Layla had pressed for details and found out that Nick Thurston had recommended her for a make-up position at a local theater company. Layla ordered her to take it for two reasons: a job was a job in the off-season and the theater had a good reputation, and if Nick went to the trouble, Erin should take advantage. She hadn't asked for it so it would be insulting to dismiss it out of hand without even setting up an interview. Erin agreed and Layla toasted her with the last of the wine.

It was worth it to wake up on Sunday with a wicked case of dry mouth and a stubborn headache. After a night with a girlfriend, her heartache was lessened if not gone. She'd panicked. So what? Erin was positive that Russ liked her enough to get past it. Layla knew she had to take the first step so she showed up on Monday intending to get the apology out of the way. But the fight coordinator was nowhere to be found.

The hairdresser's advice was to leave a voicemail with a general apology for running out and a request to talk. So Layla did. He didn't respond or appear. The next day, she sent a text with the same message. Erin swore that she was sure he'd respond. He didn't. The first day Layla wanted to cry. The second, she wanted to die. This liking a guy business sucked. At least she had one friend in her corner. Erin was livid that Russ was being such an asshole but Layla wouldn't let her vent her disappointment on her preferred target. She had one friend on the set; she didn't want her to get into trouble.

Now they'd wrapped for the day, almost a full week after the date that mostly wasn't. Two attempts at communication was all that Erin said she was allowed. The next move had to come from Russ. Layla didn't know what she was going to do if he didn't make one. Unsure of what her next play should be, she decided to search out her love guru for advice.

Instead she opened her door and found even more trouble on her doorstep. Literally. Because that was her life. "Kristin, what the hell are you doing here? I fired you, remember? Or did somebody else hire you on?" Please, God, don't let her cast mates be that stupid. Chris hadn't known better at the time. At this point, there was no excuse.

"Mom said to give you a couple days to cool down. I told her the Sydney toga thing was an accident and she said you should accept my apology. She also said you'd give me Friday morning off since I have a massage appointment with Joy."

Some things never changed. "Nope, you're still

fired." Some things did. Occasionally there was a miracle of modern science and a person could spontaneously regrow a spine.

"But Mom said!"

"Mom's not here. And now, you aren't either. Go home, Kristin."

"You are so going to pay for this. I'm telling Dad," her little sister threatened.

"Go ahead. Remind him that I've been paying for almost two years already. The debt's long settled. I think the rest of you have forgotten that." Layla could see Kristin winding up again and decided to cut off the next rant at the knees. "Don't make me call security again. As amusing as that was, I don't think your reputation could take the hit."

"I hate you."

"Join the club."

Men were idiots and family sucked. Where was that other bottle of wine when she needed it? Tires squealed as Kristin threw her car into gear and hit the gas. For a second, Layla wondered how her sister had managed to get past security but the thought flew out of her head when she bumped into a woman who was not Erin coming out of the make-up trailer. Apparently her day could get worse. Who knew?

"Sydney," she said. Layla tried to be polite because she was well aware friendly wasn't going to be a possibility. Unfortunately, polite seemed out of the question as well because despite her best efforts, Layla still sounded like a bitch.

"I was looking for Chris."

She tried harder for polite. "I haven't seen him yet today." Those six words didn't have a layer of frost on them. Perhaps she could do this. Layla took a deep breath because this next sentence was going to hurt. A lot. A lot. "I'm sorry for offending you with the toga costume suggestion."

"Chris said that it wasn't your idea."

"It was my sister's. Since she was working for me at the time, she was my responsibility." She took another breath. "And I apologize for not saying hi to any of your friends at the volleyball game. I couldn't."

"You wouldn't," Sydney tried to correct her. Layla watched Sydney run her palm up her bicep as if to cover the burn scar on the back of her arm.

"I couldn't," Layla stressed.

"Couldn't be seen with less than perfect people. I get it."

She knew where Sydney was coming from, but she didn't want to have this conversation in public so she waved the other woman into the make-up trailer. The accusation was perfectly rational from the Sydney's point of view. She couldn't know that it wasn't the injuries that Layla was afraid of. It was the memory of the scent of bandages and ointment, and the sound of nurses' shoes squeaking on the tile floor, and the whimpers even morphine couldn't silence. Layla had tried to visit Sydney once in the hospital after the accident but hadn't made it into the lobby. Then the lawyers found out and told her not to do it again because it could violate the gag order if anyone saw. But nobody else was here right now to see and if she were very lucky, she might be able to explain why she'd never shown up to apologize in person. "I don't care about the scars. I never did. I just can't do hospitals. Not after my dad. I can't. I'm sorry. I'm sorry for the accident. I'm sorry you were hurt. I'm sorry I didn't visit to say so. I'm sorry, Sydney."

That was it. That was everything she had. Layla

wasn't selfless enough to take the blame for the parts that weren't her fault but she finally got a chance to apologize for the pieces of the tragedy that were. As much as she wanted Sydney to forgive her, she was done.

Sydney said nothing at all. She stared. Layla refused to blink. The silence drew out until the trailer door flew open and banged against the aluminum siding. Locks of hair stuck to the sides if Erin's sweating face. "Where have you been? You need to go to the hospital. There's been an accident."

Layla felt the blood drain out of her face as she remembered the screeching tires. "Kristin?"

Erin shook her head. "Russ."

Somebody sucked all the air out of the room. How rude was that? Layla decided – well, her body decided – to sit on the floor. It seemed to think there would be more oxygen at a lower altitude.

"What's wrong with her?" Sydney asked the stylist.

"She and Russ are dating," Erin replied.

"Not dating," Layla managed to say between gasps.

"Mostly dating except Russ is being a jerk at the moment." Erin grabbed Layla's forearms and tugged. "On your feet, Hera. We can follow the ambulance in my car."

"I am not going to the hospital!"

"Yes, you are." The fingers around her wrists tightened. "Jesus, Layla, are you breathing?"

And then she was in the trailer, sitting in the make-up chair.

"Layla, you still with us?"

"I'm not going to a hospital. I'm not."

Layla heard the pop-hiss-fizz of a soda can being opened. "I'm starting to get that," Sydney said. She handed Layla the cold can but had to wrap her fingers around Layla's to keep her from dropping it. "Drink. You're in shock."

She had no idea what it was. Layla drank until Sydney pulled away the can.

Erin took her hands and chaffed them between her own. "Layla, we need to get going. Don't you want to make sure Russ is okay?"

Layla nodded.

"We have to go to the hospital to do that."

The actress shook her head.

"Okay. How about we get some air then?"

Air was good. She liked air. Besides, there was something wrong with the temperature in the make-up trailer. It must have been blasting heat before the air-conditioning kicked into overdrive because her shirt was soaked through and she was freezing. Layla leaned on the railing. It wasn't significantly warmer outside but there was a breeze. And there was air.

"Erin's back with her car," Sydney told her.

Layla's first question was when did Erin leave? Her second was why on earth was Chris' girlfriend being so nice? Sydney hated her. She didn't hate her for the right reasons but hate was hate and this kindness was throwing her right off. "That means you have to let go of the hand rail," Sydney continued.

"Why?"

"So you can go check on your boyfriend."

Layla shook her head again. "I can't."

"If you care for him at all, get in the fucking car, Layla. Get your ass to the hospital."

Russ was probably there already. He'd be gasping for breath with an oxygen tube up his nose and the cloying stink of disinfectants and medicine coating everything like a layer of malignant grime. He'd want to hold her hand to say goodbye but needles in his veins would keep him from being able to curl his fingers around hers so they'd just lie limply in her palm. The machines would beep, then scream, and the nurses would push her out of the room—

If nothing else, trying to breathe after she finished throwing up snapped her back to reality. Thank God the stairs were metal grates and not something that was going to need much washing off.

"Wow, you really weren't kidding," Sydney commented as she handed Layla the same can from earlier. "You done?"

Layla swished the liquid around in her mouth and spat it onto the pavement. At this point it didn't matter. "Sure."

Sydney stared at her for a minute. "Are you going to let go of the railing then?"

The hand not holding the can still had a death grip on the metal bar. Layla focused on it until her white knuckles relaxed enough for her to peel her fingers away. Her stomach flipped again when she reached the bottom step but there was nothing left.

"Jesus. At least you'll be empty for the drive."

* * * *

This was humiliating. He'd been impaled by an arrowhead. In the back of his upper thigh. Really upper. Russ could not believe that he'd stuck himself in the ass with one of Eros' arrows. Sean had even warned him that he'd set the quiver on the bench. He'd needed a tetanus shot. And stitches. There wasn't enough money in the world to keep this from getting to the guys in his former unit. They'd made it through two tours in the Sandbox and were going to die laughing on American soil. There was no possible happy ending for this afternoon.

At least his butt wasn't flapping in the wind. He owed Nick a beer since the actor had thoughtfully grabbed a pair of track pants on the rush to the hospital. The nurse helped him put them on after they cut off his jeans. It was the least the god of war could have done considering Nick was the reason he was on set in the first place. Russ had been trying to teach Nick the footwork he'd need for an upcoming swordfight but the actor just wasn't getting it. The guy had two left feet, possibly three.

Russ hadn't been at his best either. It was getting harder to keep himself from calling Layla. He'd started taking the long way around to avoid her trailer because his big brother's advice was killing him. She said she shouldn't have run out of the restaurant without talking to him. Russ didn't want to have a talk with her. He'd heard some of her talks and Layla had left her victims bleeding and speechless. He felt bad enough already, although she did deserve a target. He was too cowardly and not willing to give up his good memories of her when the queen bitch of Olympus made her triumphant return. But he missed her.

He could practically hear her voice now, which was strange because they hadn't given him any good drugs beyond a little injection of Lidocaine for numbing the area for the eight stitches they put in his butt cheek.

"God, you're not going to throw up again, are you?" a familiar female voice said from the other side of the curtain.

"Throw up what? There's nothing left," imaginary Layla said. Then the curtain zinged back along the track to reveal a violently trembling Filipino firecracker being propped up by a somewhat nervous hairdresser. "Hi, Russ."

Jesus, she looked worse than he did. Layla's face was covered with a sheen of sweat and her rosy cheeks were unnaturally pale. Actually, her whole golden brown complexion had an unhealthy green tinge to it. Her usual chocolate irises looked smaller and surrounded by more white than normal as she blinked rapidly, to say nothing about the fact that she was holding on to Erin like her life depended on it. "What are you doing here?"

"Erin said you got hurt on the set."

"Hurt, yes. But I'm not dying."

Totally the wrong thing to say. Layla shook herself loose from Erin's grip and darted down the hall. He heard plastic clatter off the tiled floor and the unmistakable sounds of heaving. "Nice one, Russ. There goes the water," the hairdresser said.

Layla limped back to his cubicle. "Sorry. Are you okay? Can I do anything for you?"

Knife. In the heart. He was such an asshole. "No, I'm good. They're just about to release me." He looked over at Nick, then to Erin. "Can you guys give us a minute?"

They disappeared but Layla didn't move any closer to the bed. He propped himself up on his elbows and decided he owed Nick two beers since his bare ass wasn't exposed for his sort-of girlfriend to see while he was lying on his stomach. That was not the impression he wanted to make when she saw him naked for the first time. "Layla, can you come over here for a minute?" She shook her head. The curtain hooks rattled at the same time. Then he realized that she had the curtain in a death-grip just to stay upright. He didn't know how that was even possible. "I'm happy you came but should you even be here? This is a hospital."

"Believe me, I know. Erin said you were hurt. Ambulance-worthy hurt. I couldn't not come."

Knife. Twisting. "The restaurant was a disaster. It wasn't your fault." If she could face her greatest fear, the least he could do was admit his mistake. Why was he listening to Leo in the first place? If his big brother were that great with women, he wouldn't still be single.

"It's okay."

"Can we try it again then?"

She pinched her lips shut but managed to nod. Then her hand dropped to her stomach again.

"Look, I'm really not that injur—"

She was gone. Nick stepped back into the cubicle. "Erin's got her." He stepped closer to the bed. "You're dating the bitch queen?" he asked quietly, as if he were afraid of being overheard. Actually, Nick probably was afraid. Layla had earned her reputation on the set and despite the improvement over the last couple weeks it was going to be around for a long time.

"One date so far. Maybe another one if I get lucky."

"And have you gotten lucky?"

No way was he answering that question. Be an asshole once, shame on him. Be one twice and lose all hope of ever having sex with the most gorgeous woman on the planet. "Can you find a doctor and see if I can go home now?"

"He came by while you we talking with Layla. You already signed the paperwork so he dropped off the prescription. I have the chair to wheel you out. Look, they even gave you one of those ass donut cushions they give to people with hemorrhoids." The actor spun a wheelchair around the curtain and the plastic tires squeaked on the floor. "I'll be careful. No speed bumps or wheelies, I promise."

"Do you have somebody to stay with you?" Layla asked. She was back but her breathing was even shallower than it had been before.

"I don't need anybody. I'll be okay. I like standing anyway," Russ said.

"Again, glad you're not an actor," Layla tried to joke. "You look like you're in pain." She pressed her lips together and swallowed hard.

"For God's sake, Layla, I'll meet you outside. Get out of here before you pass out." Russ' words sounded harsh, but the light in his eyes said he was happy for her presence.

"You can't be alone. What if you have a concussion?" Layla asked, repeating his concerns from her attack.

Nick snorted. "Layla, he stabbed himself in the ass."

But Russ had to smile at the same line he used on her. He sucked at apologizing and she wasn't much for granting forgiveness. This might be as close as the two of them could get. "I live by myself but I'll be fine," Russ said, trying to sound extra pitiful.

"Maybe you should stay at my place tonight. Just in case," she offered. A machine started squealing down the hall and a herd of interns and nurses thundered by. Layla wrapped her arms around her stomach, practically doubling over on herself. "I'll wait outside." Erin hefted Layla upright by her collar and raced for the exit.

"I could drive you over to your brother's place. Or your other brother's place. Or your other other brother's. Or, you know, anywhere the worst person on the planet doesn't live," Nick offered with a laugh.

"Shut up."

Chapter 9

Layla dropped the empty tube of toothpaste into the garbage can beside the empty bottle of mouthwash. She hadn't thrown up in forty minutes, a new record. Russ was passed out on her bed, face down and sprawled all over her bamboo pillow cases and sheets. The pain pills had finally kicked in and he was out for the count.

She'd had more visitors to her apartment in the last month than she'd had in the last two years. Erin drove her home, which unfortunately left her car on the lot overnight. Nick Thurston and Russ were about ten minutes behind them, having stopped at the hospital pharmacy first. It gave her time to change the bedding before they arrived. It would be her turn to spend the night on the couch.

She was really glad she'd gone to the hospital. Whatever had been between her and Russ had definitely moved into relationship territory. It was apparent that Erin had kept her mouth shut about Layla's burgeoning romance since the biggest gossip on the set hadn't had a clue. Unfortunately he had one now. Nick would spread the news far and wide by the time she showed up tomorrow.

Surprisingly, she wasn't that pissed at the idea. She was more upset that he wouldn't have much to gossip about because Russ wasn't going to be up for anything for a while. It was probably for the best. They shouldn't go too fast. They'd only had one date, and not even a whole one at that.

Who was she kidding? She was ready to jump him now, injured or not. He was six feet of yummy goodness under that cropped black hair and he was already in her bed. It had been difficult enough working with him for the last couple years when all she could do was look but recently having had more than one chance to feel the six-pack under his shirt, she wanted to do it with no clothing between them.

Layla slipped into her bedroom and drew the comforter over his still body, trying not to wake him. "It's okay," his muffled voice said through the pillow. "I'm up."

"Sorry," she whispered as she tried to sneak out of the room.

"Don't go. Talk to me."

"You should go back to sleep."

"The shot's wearing off. I need a distraction," the ass-kicking fight choreographer whined.

Layla sat on the edge of the bed, fists in her lap. The poor guy looked uncomfortable and tense as hell. She would have offered him a backrub to help him fall back asleep, but she wasn't certain she could keep her hands from wandering.

Russ raised his head off the pillow. "I can't talk to you way over there. My neck hurts."

She gently lay down on the mattress and rested her cheek on the cool pillowcase on the other side of the bed. "You should be sleeping." She kept her voice soft and low.

"Why did you do that?"

She frowned. Perhaps the pills were stronger than she thought. "You said you wanted me to talk to you."

"To the hospital. Why did you come?"

Layla snuggled deeper into the pillow. "What? I can't check on a friend?"

His voice got deep. Deep and serious. It did things to her. Naughty things. His dark brown eyes pinned her down like she was prey caught in his sights and escape didn't seem to be her first pick. "I don't think that's why you came. Was it?"

What was the question again? "Maybe I didn't want the last thing between us to be some stupid fight."

"I wasn't dying, Layla."

"Erin made it sound like you were." Her stomach started to gurgle again and she curled up, pulling her knees tight to her chest to hide the sound. She was already sore from all the puking. She needed a little time to level everything out. "I had to make sure I got a chance to say goodbye."

Russ wormed his hand along her side until it was pressed against her shirt. "I saw what it did to you. I'm sorry."

His palm was hot against her skin. The heat of it seeped in and started to melt the block of ice in her chest that had frozen when Erin had first made her announcement. "Just don't do anything like that again. I can go another twenty years without a hospital visit, thank you."

"I'll do my best. Tired now." Russ closed his eyes.

It sounded like a promise. Everyone knows a promise should be sealed with something. Layla carefully propped herself on an elbow and stretched until she could reach Russ's pillow. She didn't blink as she lowered her head until she could put a soft kiss on his lips.

* * * *

Russ pulled the sleeping Queen of Olympus a little closer. Layla curled into him and her warm breath brushed over his shoulder. At least one of them was getting some rest. A raging hard-on while he was forced to sleep on his stomach was no fun at all.

He couldn't believe she'd shown up at the emergency room. She'd told him how much she hated hospitals but he didn't think anyone had any idea exactly how deep her fear went. Nick had been astounded at the sheer amount of vomit the tiny actress was able to produce. Since the story was going to get out anyway, Russ didn't feel bad sharing Layla's father's history. Nick hid his emotions pretty well but some sympathy seemed to appear on the drive to her apartment.

That was just his luck too. This was his second sleepover with the girl of his dreams and he hadn't made it to second base yet. Hell, if it weren't for that pity goodnight peck he tricked out of her he wouldn't even be stranded on first. Reluctantly, he admitted he wasn't in any shape to go any further but he was willing to try.

One thing was certain. Two things. He was never going to his eldest brother for advice again. Secondly, there was definitely something going on between him and Layla. Something much bigger than he initially suspected. He knew how he felt; he'd been near-obsessively attracted to her for years. That was just physically. She wore her hair loose while she slept. Russ wrapped the end of a curl around his finger and stroked the silky strands. Layla fought the stereotypes on every level. Yes, she was tiny but there was nothing doll-like about her. Nothing fragile to be spotted as a weakness.

Getting to know her on the personal side just added to the attraction because that's where her softness lay. He couldn't blame her for the armor she wore to protect herself when every time she turned around he found something else she was protecting herself from.

It killed him that he added to her hurt, even a little bit. He wouldn't do it again. The hospital trip had proven that she'd share if he gave her the time. She could have all the time she wanted as long as she kept him close like this.

Actually, he'd prefer a bit closer but that was for another day when he could show her how much he appreciated her trust.

Chapter 10

Her stomach fluttered. Not nervous butterfly flutters either, but plain hurt after the workout she gave her abs yesterday. Layla didn't mean to but she pulled a mild bitch face to hide her discomfort as she climbed out of Erin's car. She really owed her friend for picking her up in Los Angeles in morning rush hour. The chill she'd been fighting since Kristin's reappearance yesterday returned with a vengeance the second her foot hit the pavement. It was in the air.

It wasn't only her either. Erin came around her car with a pensive look on her face. "What's up?"

"I don't know," Layla admitted. But it scared her. Generally she was the cause of tension but she hadn't done anything this time. She thought for a minute, trying to think of anything that Nick could have misconstrued but came up blank. "I don't like it."

She greeted Sean and Nick on the walk from the parking lot. They offered hellos and small waves but spun off in another direction before she could talk to them. Before now, Sean's cold shoulder had thawed noticeably over the last couple weeks. It didn't bode well that he brushed her off this morning.

Chris Peck was standing outside her trailer, a folded newspaper in hand. He didn't look pleased. Layla knew why too. Her scene with Sydney had to have upset her as much as it had Layla. Sydney and Chris hadn't been dating long but the king of the gods definitely had a protective streak for the woman he once had to serve.

"It wasn't me. Or Sydney," he said.

"What wasn't?" Layla asked. His tone was defensive. Maybe a little sorry too. This was not the Zeus she knew.

"You haven't seen it?"

Layla noticed the crowd starting to gather and pointed to her door. "Inside." Chris handed her the paper and silently followed her inside. He leaned against the counter while Layla dropped onto the sofa and scanned the headlines on the front page and then flipped deeper into the paper. The cover photo was one of her losing her lunch on the stairs the day before with Sydney looking on, concern evident on her face. The headline was just as unflattering "Morning Sickness for Olympus's Hera – Who's the Daddy?"

She felt the full force ice queen mask slide into place when she got to the article. The one that said how her BFF and costar's girlfriend, Sydney Richardson, was helping her through her journey to single motherhood since she wasn't talking about who the father was. Then she got to the part where her hormones were so out of control that she attacked the show's fight coordinator and sent him to the hospital after a bad take. Rumor had it that she got him fired too.

Layla wanted to tear the paper into itty bitty pieces and stomp on them, yelling till she was hoarse. Really wanted to. Instead she folded it and set it on the table between her and Chris. "Is it too early for alcohol?"

He snorted once. Then he got serious again. "It wasn't us. Sydney says you weren't having morning sickness."

"Soooo not pregnant. Don't worry, I know it wasn't her. She'd never talk to the press."

"I am a little curious about the part about Russ. I know you two were fighting. Is that why he's not coming back?"

"Not coming back? Where's he going?" That worm never said a word about leaving last night. Sure, he was medicated to the gills but he could have hinted that he'd taken the new job offer.

"You didn't know he was leaving?" Chris moved closer, perching on the arm of the sofa.

"I knew he had another offer on the table but he never said he'd made a decision." God, this was probably why he'd been dodging her all week. He didn't think they could work together after the pico de gallo disaster. Then she forced him into spending the night at her place and he couldn't refuse without making her look bad in front of everybody at the hospital so he went along with it. No wonder he said he'd wait for his brother to pick him up rather than drive in with her and Erin. She was such an idiot.

Chris was talking again. "What was that?" she asked.

"You knew he was thinking about leaving?" the actor repeated. "Do you know why?"

"It didn't have anything to do with me," Layla protested. "It was a family thing. Russ asked me not to say anything so if you want more information you should ask him."

He tried the death stare, the one that he used to try to put her in her place when she was the bitch queen on a regular basis. It worked as well for him now as it had then. "Okay, I'll ask him when I see him." He pointed to her fridge and opened it when she gave him the nod and pulled out a bottled water. "Any idea when that might be?"

She shook her head. "His brother was picking him up later this morning." Layla flipped over the paper to take another look at the front page, and then turned it face down again. "I suppose I should call Martine."

Martine Peeples was the show's public relations person. She handled all things media. Well, all official things media. Layla was about to ruin her morning. Martine wasn't obligated to help but she'd be inclined since it was her job to preserve the show's public face in any circumstances. Plus, to make up for her lack of participation on the show's media sites, Layla had been feeding her information on her support of various local children's drama groups for the last two years. Layla knew how to play the game. Granted, Martine hadn't done very much with it but Layla had given her options.

"She already knows. Expect a call."

"Great. Thanks." Then another thought hit her. "How's Sydney with all this BFF bullshit?"

"Not pleased. Neither are her friends, by the way, but she said the same thing you did. She knew it wasn't you." Chris played with the bottle cap for a moment. "She also said you apologized. I don't know what for, she didn't say." His nose turned up at that last line. Layla could only imagine the horrible scenarios running through his head, like his girlfriend and his nemesis getting together and painting each other's toes.

"Don't worry, she still hates me," Layla said.

The awkward pause ended with a knock on the door. Martine appeared as if summoned, with a Bluetooth attached to her ear and an oversized purse on her shoulder. The gorgeous blonde was done up to the nines in a four-figure suit and perfect hair and make-up. No matter what time of day an emergency hit, she always looked flawless. "Layla, do you have a minute?"

"She does. I'm leaving." Sure, after dropping half a dozen bombshells on her, although they weren't malicious bombshells.

This new Chris Peck would bear watching.

* * * *

It was like waking up after a drunken brawl without

the fun beforehand. Only it was less of a headache and more of a pain in the ass. He hurt. Not only from the arrow wound but from torqueing his back as he'd fallen off the bench. He vaguely remembered Layla saying good-bye when she'd left for work. His phone was plugged in on the breakfast bar beside a post-it telling him that there were bagels and cream cheese in the fridge and coffee ready to be made once he hit the switch.

Layla really was a goddess. A goddess of Kona. Russ normally didn't care where the coffee came from as long as it was hot and black. He'd grown up on the store-brand special and then whatever they served in the navy. He liked this stuff much better.

He was on his third cup when Leo showed up. "This is it?" Leo asked as he looked around the apartment.

Russ tried to see what his brother did but he couldn't. "What?"

"Couldn't she hire that guy to do one of those four-in-one portrait dealios above the sofa? She can afford it. And you'd think an actress would have more mirrors. Wait a minute – where's her bedroom? I need to check out the ceiling."

"He's dead." Leo shot him a look. "Andy Warhol did the Marilyn Monroe Diptych those paintings are based on. He's dead," Russ elaborated.

"Look at you, Mr. Art History minor."

"You know, I was going to offer you a cup of Layla's primo coffee but we'll be going now."

Since he was still medicated and couldn't drive himself, Leo took them back to his office. Their office. Russ passed out on the sofa, dozing while Leo and Marcus Bolling debated if they wanted to bring in Leo's buddy as a fourth partner.

"Russ, wake up, buddy," the Texan rumbled. "Your

pants are ringing."

By the time Russ had found his pant pocket where his phone was hiding and pulled it out, he caught a flash of Layla's name before the call went to voicemail. "Fuck!" The expletives continued when he saw the two other missed calls from her. The first warned him about the article in the tabloid that said he'd been fired from the show; she assured him he hadn't been. The second congratulated him on his new job and requested that he call Martine Peeples to get some kind of press release quote. But the third one…the third one killed him. She thanked him for accepting her apology and promised never to bring it up again. She wouldn't bother him anymore and would see him at work the next time they had a fight to block.

Layla didn't answer when he called. He didn't waste time trying again. Instead he went directly to the source of all gossip. "Nick, man, what's happening over there? I'm away for one day…"

"Don't worry, you're not fired."

"Layla told me. What's going on?"

"She's also not pregnant."

"What?" He pictured the wince on Nick's face since he yelled that last bit into the phone.

"She's not pregnant," Nick repeated. "Didn't she tell you that part?"

"She didn't tell me she wasn't not pregnant." Damn, all the negatives were getting confusing. "Who said she was pregnant?" Russ asked.

"Tabloids. The same one that said you were fired. None of it's true. They did get a shot of her puking her guts up outside her trailer so it made for a good headline," Nick clarified.

"I missed her call. Is Layla around?" Please let her

still be around, Russ thought.

"No, she's gone. What the hell's going on with you guys? You went home with her but she said your brother was picking you up. Are you two fighting or dating or what? Inquiring minds, my friend."

"Yes. No. I don't know," Russ admitted.

"Oh, this is gonna be good!" Nick laughed before he hung up.

"Shit. Shit. Fuck!" He'd worked his ass off making sure he stayed away from Layla and she'd gotten the message. But she'd gotten it too late. There wasn't a lot of forgiveness in her and he wasn't sure he deserved it anyway.

He regrouped. If Layla could apologize, he could. Of course, he needed an apology that couldn't be ignored. Yeah, he'd shame her into giving him a second chance if he had to. He wouldn't waste it either because with what he knew of her past, there was no way in hell he'd ever get a third.

Chapter 11

Layla couldn't get clean. She'd drowned in the looks and whispers all day long. Martine was good at her job but nobody wanted to hear the truth when the lies were so much juicier. Even a scalding hot shower hadn't helped. She still felt like the gum somebody had scraped off their shoe. One thing had become blatantly clear; Russ was adored at his job. He was more popular than she was.

Her only saving grace was the fact that her parents obviously hadn't seen the article yet. She'd broken her radio silence to send a single text to her mother before shutting off her phone for the night. *BUSY AT WORK. SEE YOU FOR SUPPER ON SUNDAY. LOVE, LAYLAY.* That would get her off the hook for tomorrow and then she'd ignore everything else till Sunday because they were certain to have heard the rumors by then. Of course, it also meant she had to show up for supper on Sunday. Lose some, lose some.

She could have died. He showed up with a bouquet of lilies and a box of fruit jellies. Not roses and not chocolates. How long had he been paying attention? Layla shook her head. She didn't want to know. She didn't know what game he was playing but she knew her luck with him had run out. Experience had taught her it didn't hurt as much to leave the game when she left the table early. After a lifetime of losing, she'd become a quick learner.

"Can I help you?" she asked, barring the way with one hand on the door frame and one just above the deadbolt.

Russ' grin faltered. "Can I come in so we can talk?"

"Was there something you needed?"

"Yeah." Then he stopped talking. Layla had to admit

that it was an effective trick since she wasn't about to have a conversation with him in the corridor. Reluctantly she stepped aside and he slipped between her and the doorframe. Her grip on the door tightened when he brushed his hand across her cheek as he passed.

He set the flowers and candy on the breakfast bar and then took off his jacket and dumped it on a stool. He seemed to be making himself at home. It looked pretty good on him too. Damn him. She'd gotten used to having him around after less than a week.

"What was it you needed?" she asked.

Russ carefully lowered himself onto the center sofa cushion. "I need you to accept my apology. Two of them, actually."

Layla felt confusion draw her eyebrows together. "You haven't done anything that needs an apology."

He leaned forward, elbows on his knees. "I pushed at the restaurant. I shouldn't have. You asked me not to and I should have respected your boundaries. I'm sorry."

Hot damn. A straight-out apology for fucking up. It was impressive. It didn't change anything but it was impressive. "It's okay."

"It's really not. Because after acting like an ass I doubled-down and ignored you instead of manning up. I'm sorry for that too."

"Okay?" This was nice but she didn't quite know what to do with it.

"So, if you've forgiven me, I thought you might kiss me again." He looked up at her, not far up because even standing when he was sitting there wasn't much of a difference, and let loose a slow, sexy smile that made her feel like she was bursting into flames all over.

"What?" she squeaked.

Russ patted the cushion beside him. "It wasn't really

fair, you know. A sneak attack like that. I wasn't ready to respond. I can do a hell of a lot better. I'm sorry, Layla. Can we try to redo the ending to last Friday? I didn't even get a good night kiss." When she didn't move, he did. He stood up and hovered over her. "I'd really like a good night kiss, Layla."

He leaned over in slow motion and Layla watched as his lips got closer. The second they touched hers, though, she closed her eyes and lost herself in the kiss. Russ knew what he was doing. God, did he know.

The heat from his lips and his hands on her hips spread like wildfire as his touch moved to her back. He slid his hands under her ass and lifted her high enough to wrap her legs around his waist. "Watch the stitches," he murmured. Then Layla gently ran the tips of her nails up the back of his neck and wove her fingers into his short black hair and he forgot all about them.

He stood there for ages, tasting her and letting her taste him back. Then he took two steps to the sofa and turned, pinning her back to the cushions and covering her with his body like a cage. He kept his weight on his forearms but allowed himself to stay pressed against her.

"If I'd know you kissed like that, I never would have been able to stay away for two years," he breathed.

"Likewise."

"So this is our second date, right? I can go for second base."

Layla shook her head and he groaned. "Third date," she corrected. "No, fourth. You've already slept over twice."

His smile was blinding.

"I'm not saying you're going to make it past third tonight, buster."

"I am going to make it all the way home," he

promised

Then he kissed her again to prove it.

* * * *

His little firecracker put out heat like a furnace. Russ flipped the duvet off, leaving just the sheet covering him. Layla snuggled closer, one hand on his side stroking his ribs even as she slept. They'd moved from making out in the living room to making love in the bedroom somewhere between her bra and his boxers coming off. Even though he'd had to be careful of his injury, it hadn't slowed them down in the slightest. They'd fallen asleep hours later, and the sun peeking in through the blinds in Layla's bedroom was what had woken him up now. The streams of sunlight hit him square in the face.

"Good morning," Layla whispered. When he said nothing back, a shadow crossed her face, giving her a look that was a little lost and uncertain.

Russ rolled till she was underneath him again and kissed her. He meant to keep it light but tongues—and then hands—started moving and before he knew it, it was the best kind of good morning.

"It is now," he finally said once he caught his breath.

Then Layla kissed him, short and sweet. "I hate to say it but I have to get up and get to work."

He growled. "I'm off on disability."

"Are you coming back at all?" she asked.

The small voice was back. He didn't like it. "Of course I'm coming back. It's only a flesh wound," he joked.

"What about the job with your brother's company?"

"I still have ten weeks before we even have to think about it. After that we have as long as we want. I just won't be on set all the time."

"So you are thinking longer than ten weeks for us?"

"Hell, yeah."

Her head dropped to his chest and her shoulders relaxed. His did too. He didn't like games and was surprised but relieved to realize Layla didn't either. They'd been dancing around each other for two years already. Now that they'd taken the first step, they seemed to be in agreement that they wanted to go for the second.

"We seem to fight a lot."

"We make up a lot too. That's the fun part." She didn't return his smile at that. "Seriously, though, next time I'll back off when you tell me to drop a conversation. Just don't lie. That's why I called it off with my last girlfriend."

She nodded slowly. "In case we still aren't fighting by the weekend, do you want to come to a birthday supper with me on Sunday?"

"Whose birthday?"

"My mom's. I know it's pretty quick but…"

"Yes." He'd already met Kristin. The rest of her family couldn't be any worse, and if they were she needed protection.

"Work," Layla repeated, drawing out the word into a zombie-like groan.

Russ kissed the top of her head and then carefully rolled away. "You go ahead. I'll just laze around here while you get ready."

"That attitude is going to get you a spanking."

Russ quickly covered the bandage on his butt cheek. "Not funny!"

Chapter 12

Layla looked at the name on the script of next week's episode and set it down without opening it. She knew it was going to be bad, mostly because she had pissed the screenwriter off twice in the last two years and although they didn't have much power, writers did have the ability to craft some awful payback. She didn't have the strength to deal with what was between the covers and handle her family on the same day so she decided to fight the bigger battle first. She couldn't change the words on the page anyway.

For Christmas, she and her sisters had bought a charm bracelet for their mother. Today, Layla was giving her a new charm, and a set of customized bath oils. No doubt Kristin and Joy would be giving her charms too, but Layla refused to divulge her source for her other gift. The twins would have to come up with their own ideas. Russ panicked at the thought of a gift but Layla assured him that a bouquet of flowers would be just fine.

She didn't want to take any chances about Russ not being welcomed so she broke down and called her mom directly to tell her she was bringing a date to dinner. She'd gotten lucky. Her mother was so thrilled with the news that she was dating that she didn't have time to bring up anything else before Layla ended the call.

Layla tugged on her shirt-dress, trying to pull out the creases that were forming in the amethyst fabric. She couldn't go home in jeans; her mother would kill her. But this was supposed to be a relaxed family dinner so the casual dress was a compromise. Also, it was too late to change since Russ was waiting at the curb.

It had been a while since she'd been to her parents' house, she thought as they pulled into the driveway. It hadn't been home for over a year now, not because she'd moved out but because she'd stopped feeling welcome.

"Did you warn them about the article?" Russ' rumbling voice jarred her back to the present.

"Yeah."

"Do you know who spoke to the press?"

"No. But the facts that Kristin snuck onto the lot just before everything went down and that she's pissed at me are pointing to some place I don't want to think about. My parents don't know that part so please don't say anything."

"Fair enough. Are we going to go in? I'm good with sitting in the car. You look great and we can see how far I can slide my hand up your skirt before I have to start unbuttoning it. But someone is watching us from the living room," he added, indicating the window in question.

"On second thought…"

"Out of the truck, Layla."

Things went spectacularly well. At first. She introduced Russ to everyone he hadn't met, and Angelo Aquino was very impressed at Russ' naval service. Her mother, Mariel, was thrilled with the flowers. Layla's youngest sister Joy perched on the arm of a chair near the kitchen and worked her way through a couple cans of cola. Layla sat between Russ and her grandfather while her mother opened presents in the living room. After every one, the elderly man would yell, "What is that?" and she'd shout back in his ear "Perfume, lolo" or "Jewelry, po."

Then came dinner. Joy stopped behind Russ and filled his wine glass. He simply moved it in front of her and took her empty one. "You can have a glass if you want," she whispered.

"No, I can't. Antibiotics. You enjoy, I'm driving."

"Layla's not allowed to drink," Joy stated, reaching between them and removing the full wine glass.

"Why not?" Russ asked.

Layla felt herself turn half a dozen shades of red. "I can have a glass, Joy."

Her sister leered at her as she gulped down half the contents from Layla's glass. "No you can't. She has a drinking problem, doesn't she, Tatay?" Joy giggled.

"No, I don't." This wasn't happening. It couldn't be. Layla looked to her step-father but he refused to meet her gaze. Her mother dropped the casserole dish full of pinakbet on the table and ran back into the kitchen. Layla couldn't breathe; her parents were going to let Joy throw her under the bus. Again. She looked at Russ and couldn't keep the tremor out of her voice. "I don't."

"I believe you." Russ reached over, grabbed her hand and gave it a squeeze.

Joy slouched against the side board, grinning as her mother's birthday party deteriorated into an ugly family fight. "You shouldn't. Perfect little Laylay was convicted of driving her car through a window into a restaurant. She got eighteen months of probation. She's lucky they didn't tack on a driving while impaired charge. She almost killed a girl. I think you know her – Sydney Richardson?"

Russ' fingers froze, then he slowly peeled them away from her. "I assumed you were involved. I thought you were in the car, not driving."

"I was." She realized what it sounded like and tried to explain but the slack look on her date's face told her it was already too late. "I was in the car. I wasn't driving."

Joy slammed the wine glass down on the table and leaned into Layla's face. "You can't say that, Laylay. Tatay, tell her she's not allowed to say anything to her hottie."

Then Layla understood, breathing in a cloud reeking of cola and rum fumes under the red wine. "Joy, you're drunk," she said quietly.

"I'm not drunk! Drunk, ha!"

"You're drunk. Just like you were drunk that night. And all the other times you drove."

"Laylay!" That came from her step-father but she didn't have time to address him. She was trying to dodge her sister's roundhouse swing. For once, Joy's alcoholic tendencies worked in Layla's favor because Russ grabbed the incoming fist and twisted until Joy's torso lay flat against the table top, squishing plates and shoving silverware to the floor.

"Oh my God, oh my God!"

She wasn't sure who was shouting. In the end, it didn't matter. Layla shoved her chair back and stood up. "I can't do this anymore. She needs help." Her mother peeked in from the kitchen. "Sorry, Nanay, but we can't stay. Get her into rehab."

"We will," her step-father promised.

"I've heard that before. Do it this time before she kills somebody. She's unsafe." It was so hard to see her baby sister like this. Hard and scary and humiliating and hatefully rage-inducing. Every fear, every regret, every insult she'd swallowed and choked on since the accident threatened to slip out of the box she'd forced them into and explode, taking down the few pieces of her world that were still standing. It took everything she had but she held her tongue, not speaking at all for fear she would never be able to stop.

Russ kept Joy pinned until Layla was clear of the room. Then he let her little sister go and stepped back. Joy swung at him again but got caught in the chair legs.

She went down in a heap, cursing Layla and Russ, and the rest of her family.

Russ didn't say a word as they hurried out of the house and climbed into the cab of his truck. He didn't say a word as they navigated out of the suburban development with all of its houses with the prominent garage doors that became so popular in the nineties. He didn't say a word until he yanked on the wheel and pulled into a gas station parking lot just before they hit the freeway.

"Explain," was the word he finally said.

*

What the fuck was that? It was inevitable that everybody at some point would be exposed to a date's family drama but Russ had never witnessed a meltdown like the one he'd just seen. He'd tried to stay out of it when Joy announced Layla's involvement in Sydney's accident but found himself drawn in when Layla had denied some of the charges, but not all of them. Now he had questions but he wasn't sure if the answers were going to make him feel better or not.

"Explain to me what happened back there and how it relates to Sydney's accident."

"I'm not supposed to talk about it. There's a gag order from the court."

"I think we can agree Joy blew that to hell. I won't say anything. Tell me, Layla, because what happened can't be any worse than what I'm imagining." The pieces he had made a scary picture. The parts she filled in would decide if it became Munch's Scream or just a really freaky Escher.

"A year and a half ago I was out for dinner and I had a glass of red wine," Layla began in a quiet monotone. "Then my date spilled the rest of the bottle on me accidentally. He was in no shape to drive me home and one glass put me at the legal limit so I did the right thing and called my sister to come pick me up from the restaurant."

Russ could have stopped her there. Should have. The lack of anything in her voice showed the level of emotion she was restraining but he'd asked for this and she was going to give it to him.

"I didn't know Joy had a drinking problem—" Layla cut herself off. "No more excuses or pretty words. I didn't know then that she was an alcoholic. I had no idea. I didn't smell any booze on her because I reeked of merlot. So I got in the car."

She got into the car and her sister nearly killed his friend's new girlfriend.

"I didn't even know anything was wrong until she went through the intersection without hitting the brakes. It was just BOOM! Through the front windows and into the restaurant dining room. I cracked my head on the window and stunned myself. Fortunately Joy was able to drag me out of the SUV before it caught fire. Neither of us knew that Sydney was pinned between it and a table."

Let her stop, please God. "If Joy caused the accident, why did you get convicted? That's what the probation was for, wasn't it?"

"Did you know my step-dad is a lawyer? A really good one?" she asked out of nowhere.

"No, I didn't know that."

"He is. Really good. He came down and was with Joy when she gave her statement to the police. She went first because the paramedics were still trying to talk me into going to the hospital. While I was arguing with them, Joy was telling her version of the story – the one where I was driving and the accident was all my fault. Since she was first, it became the official record. By the time it was my turn to talk to them everybody 'knew' I was the driver."

"Weren't there security cameras or anything?" Russ asked. There had to be some record of who was behind the wheel – a traffic camera or something

"No. Not that it would have made a difference. In the dark, in the rain, two little Filipino girls climbing out of the same side of a smashed up SUV? Who was going to check to see which one was driving?" Her voice showed something now, even if it was sheer exhaustion.

"Anyway, my step-dad saw that I was confused as hell and asked for a couple minutes. I told him that Joy was driving and I thought he was going to keel over in the interview room. What's the big deal? It was an accident, right? It was the truth."

The bitter Layla he knew so well was rising to the forefront. He didn't blame her but he didn't want her to make a reappearance. "Didn't he believe you?"

"Oh, he believed me. Mostly because she'd already been arrested for driving under the influence and he'd pulled in a shitload of favors to make it go away. Twice. I had no idea. If she were arrested again, she was looking at jail time, especially since other people were hurt."

Jesus. "Your dad asked you to lie?"

Layla flinched. "Not exactly. He told me what had happened and what would happen to Joy if it came out. Then he told me about a plea called "no contest". Do you know what that is?"

"It's guilty without the words." It was a lie and a cheat. The entire time Leo wore a badge, Russ heard horror stories about "no contest." It was bad enough the person didn't have the balls to come out and say they were guilty; the part that was worse was that it seldom worked unless the accused had the trifecta working for them: money, power, and fame. And Layla was telling him she played it.

"It is," she agreed. "Fortunately the wine I had kept me just under the legal limit since they tested me at the accident site so I didn't have to face a drunk driving charge. I got eighteen months of probation. That's why I've been so pissed off for the last year and a half."

"You know, I didn't know a single famous person before I started working on Olympus and, I'll be honest, a lot of you came off as entitled as hell at first. I liked you all anyway. As 'out there' as you could be, you all were there to do your jobs. You all gave a shit about the craft, as Nick would call it. I waited and watched for it but none of you flipped that switch from actor to celebrity to make excuses. Turns out, I should have started looking earlier because you've always been that way."

Tears streamed down Layla's face. "Russ—"

"Sydney could have died."

"It was an accident. I didn't run away and hide. I made a deal and took the punishment."

Russ shook his head. "It's not the same and you know it. You got probation. Your sister would have gotten a lot worse."

"What would a prison term have done? Dried her out temporarily? Joy needed help. I took the plea and Joy was supposed to take a month or however long it took in rehab to get clean. That was the deal I made with her. But right after the sentence came down my parents informed me that Joy had spoken to them and they knew they got through to her. She'd promised to stop drinking and to go to AA. They believed her. A week later I showed up for supper but Joy wasn't there. She was 'sick.' I went to her room to check on her and found her passed out. My parents knew! I washed my hands of my entire family until Kristin showed up a few months ago asking for a job. I suspected my parents put her up to it but she said it was to save money to move out. I thought she'd help me convince Joy to get help but it turns out she's as much a party girl as her twin sister."

How could he have missed this? "Sydney shouldn't pay for your sister's problems."

"She didn't. I did. How many ways can I apologize for an accident, Russ? I am sorrier that you can ever imagine that Sydney got hurt. I would have stopped it if I could but that part wasn't my fault and don't try to tell me it was. Afterwards all I was trying to do was protect my sister. I failed. Miserably. At absolutely everything. I did the best I could."

"You are such a liar."

"Yes, I am." Her voice cracked at those three little words.

He should have let it lie like she'd asked. He didn't like this Layla at all. Maybe he'd been wrong. Maybe the bitch personality wasn't as much of a mask as he'd originally thought. "I didn't think you were the type of person who would use a 'get-out-of-jail card.' I don't think I'm the type of person who can be with somebody who could hide the truth when it suits them."

Layla twisted in her seat to look at him. "What would you do to protect one of your brothers, Russ? How far would you go if you thought you were helping them?"

Russ shook his head. "Not that far." It seemed that he and Layla were destined to never make it through a date. He should have caught on the first time.

He dropped the truck back into gear and they drove to her apartment in silence. If he thought the last week on set had been awkward, the rest of the season was going to be insufferable. Maybe he could ask his boss if he could swap the rest of his contract with one of the other guys. He didn't know if he could take seeing Layla keep up her new act when he knew what was behind her mask. "About work…"

"It'll be fine. We're both professionals. I'll see you on Monday. Good-bye, Russ."

Chapter 13

She hated to do it but she'd taken a sleeping pill on Sunday night. It worked. She'd slept, long and deep and dreamlessly. That and some judiciously placed make-up were enough to erase the bags under her eyes since she hadn't slept at all on Saturday night. At least this time she'd had enough sense not to drag Erin down with her.

Her phone had gone nuts with texts and voice mails from her parents and sisters, primarily from Joy once she sobered up, begging forgiveness and swearing it was a one-time relapse and that she didn't need rehab. The ones from her parents started with pleas for her not to tell Russ – too late – and moved to promises to enroll Joy in a restricted, live-in program immediately. Layla would believe it when she saw it but she wasn't holding her breath after her last conversation with her mother.

"Laylay, I know you're still upset about what we did for Joy last time she slipped but we had to protect her."

"Yes, I'm upset. I almost went to jail and she didn't even go to rehab. You promised she'd get help."

"She doesn't need it. She just made a mistake."

"It was her third D.U.I!" Layla shouted into the phone.

"She's my little girl, Laylay."

"So am I, Nanay."

The phone calls stopped for a while after that. Then the texts and voicemails started. The only message that gave her pause was from Kristin, who called in tears. Tears of relief. "I know I'm fired but can you please call me back? I need to talk to you. Any time. Any place. You need to know something."

Considering the fact someone had provided pictures of Layla losing her lunch to the tabloids, she wasn't sure if she wanted to hear Kristin's confession. Hell, avoidance had worked just fine for the last year and a half. It could work for the next eighteen months too.

Layla caught her bitch persona sliding into place four times on the drive to the studio on Monday morning. It was a defensive reflex. She was one for two on making improvements in her social circle with her new attitude, assuming Erin stuck around after she heard about her break-up with Russ. They weren't impressive odds.

She grabbed her script and decided to pop in to see Erin before the table read. As expected, the bubbly blonde was dying for news.

"So, how was your weekend?" she drawled, lifting her eyebrows expectantly.

"Not so good. Dinner at my parents was bad. Russ found out some stuff that he decided he'd rather not have in his life so we won't be trying for a third date." She hadn't informed Erin about Russ spending the night. Layla had told herself that she wanted to keep it private. Now she admitted that she hadn't wanted the sympathy when it ended because deep down she knew it wasn't going to last.

"Stuff like?" Erin asked.

"Stuff I'd done in the past. Nothing that can be changed so the whole point is rather moot. How about you? Have you come to any professional decisions?"

Erin let her change the subject. "I called the theater and set up the interview."

"Good decision." Afraid she wasn't showing the proper enthusiasm to her friend's employment news, Layla stepped forward and opened her arms. She laughed when Erin stared at her. "Congratulatory hug," she explained.

"Holy crap, it's Armageddon. Layla Andrews is

hugging."

"Shut up."

Both women were laughing when they were interrupted by a man clearing his throat. "Shut up?" Chris Peck asked from the door.

"I was teasing her," Erin explained. "She did a good thing."

"It might have done permanent damage though," Layla joked.

Seeing Chris soured her improving mood. Since she'd already been depressed as hell on Sunday, she flipped through the current episode's pages. It was as bad as she imagined. Hera was an absolute terror to every single character and they all responded in kind. This script could undo everything she'd worked towards in the last month.

Surprisingly, the table read didn't turn out that horribly. The insults still stung, even though they were to Hera and not her, but half of them lacked the zing that would have drawn blood a week ago. It was almost as if the others were holding back too. The last thing she wanted was to draw attention to her behavior but Layla made a point of talking to the regular cast afterwards, trying to put them at ease that she wasn't her character anymore.

Then came the hard part. She, Chris, Nick and the actress who played Aphrodite all needed to work with Russ. "If you want to set a time with Russ, send me a text and I'll be there," she said to Chris.

Layla had almost made her escape when a woman she vaguely recognized approached. "Hello. You're Caitlin, right?"

"Caitlin Kelly," the black-haired woman agreed. "We didn't quite meet at the Curse the Darkness volleyball tournament."

God, shoot me now. This was one of Sydney's BFFs. Layla's first impression was made long before Caitlin ever arrived on set. "Right, I remember now. Sorry about that. Congrats on the part of Psyche."

"Sydney's mentioned you."

There was nothing Layla could say to that.

"You and Syd have your history. I'd rather make up my own with you. So thanks for the congratulations. I'm really excited to be on Olympus."

"Everybody here is great," Layla babbled, relieved beyond measure that there was one person on set who didn't hate her.

For once, Chris acted as her savior instead of her prosecutor. "Layla, Russ says now," he called from the hall.

"Coming," she shouted back. "It's nice to meet you. Again. I'm looking forward to our scenes together." Surprisingly to her, it mostly wasn't a lie.

* * * *

Russ was cool but not frostbitten. He was pretty sure that the others had no idea that he and Layla had broken up over the weekend, although Nick looked a little confused at their formality towards one another. Eventually Nick shrugged and seemed to write it off as professionalism on the job.

Layla was the first to disappear though. She hadn't called at all on Sunday. Not that he would have answered but he did check to see if she'd left any messages. Or texts. Or hang-ups.

He thought Leo would have made a joke about always listening to his big brother but the new businessman was uncharacteristically quiet at Russ' announcement. He also advised Russ not to ask to be reassigned and to finish out his contract. There was going to be a delay in getting Russ licensed which meant he'd be stuck in the office. He might as well stay where there was a good paycheck.

Besides, Russ was already working a security case, just not one for pay. He may not approve of Layla's choices but he didn't want to see her used as a punching bag either. Jeremy Bowen was still on the loose. Erin needed extra eyes on her as well. Security was as useless as fuck so he couldn't count on them.

Most of the security staff, he corrected himself. Todd Olson seemed to have pulled his head out of his ass. Russ had spotted him quite a few times in the last week, checking cars in the lot and making the rounds.

Speaking of security, he was going to have to bring his brothers through the front gate one of these days. He'd promised Leo and his middle brother Tom a tour and he had to deliver by the end of the season. Leo didn't have any burning desire to see a show being filmed but he desperately wanted to catch a glimpse of some of the actresses in togas. Including Layla, the jerk had specified with a grin.

Russ stumbled to a stop when he bumped into an object that shouldn't have been in his path. He looked down and saw Erin looking up at him, hands on her hips.

This wasn't good. "Hi, Erin. Lovely day, isn't it?"

"She's not talking," Erin informed him.

"'She' meaning Layla?" He waited for her to nod. "What isn't she talking about?"

"I don't know. Because she's not talking about it. What did she do to you that was so bad? I thought you were back together after the hospital."

"Whoa. Layla didn't do anything to me. Is that why she's saying I dumped her?"

"She's not saying anything! I told you that. You dumped her?"

Crap. If nothing else, Layla was phenomenally good at keeping her mouth shut when she wanted to. "It was mutual?"

"Sure it was."

"Can I help you with something?"

Her iciness thawed a little. "I think I saw Jeremy hanging around. I wasn't able to get close enough to tell if it was him or not. I told security but they blew me off. Again. Those sexist asshats. But since they listen to you, can you ask them to keep an eye out?"

"So you yell at me and then ask me for a favor?" Russ half-teased. Of course he'd talk to security. He didn't appreciate being raked over the coals for his personal life though.

"Of course. I learned from the queen herself."

"I'll talk to Todd."

She nodded as if to dismiss him and then walked away, which was definitely a Hera move. Maybe Layla making new friends wasn't such a good idea after all.

Chapter 14

The week continued to suck. She hated the script, she didn't get to spend much time with Erin and she had to spend extra time with Russ. In this episode Hera was the subject of an assassination attempt and damn near everybody was beating the hell out of her. Layla was truly doing her best but she wasn't getting enough sleep and the lack of it was making her slow and stupid.

The calls from home hadn't slowed down either. Unsurprisingly, Joy had talked her parents into a week's grace to "prove she could get sober by herself." Three days after that, Layla got a text from Kristin.

CAN'T REACH M/D. JOY TRASHED AT BENDERS PICK UP? K.

Layla didn't move off the couch. She did track down her parents at their bi-weekly bridge game to inform them that Joy had broken yet another promise. Layla had done her time – literally – for her sister's mistakes. If her parents were going to keep bailing her out, they were going to have to deal with her consequences.

TY. THEY GOT HER. CAN WE PLS MEET 2 TALK?

God, if Kristin had been half as persistent in doing her job as she was in begging for what she wanted, Layla wouldn't have had to fire her.

WHY? Layla texted back.

IN PERSON. ANY TIME, ANY PLC. PLS.

Tomorrow she was getting beat up again. Friday she wasn't going to be able to walk for the bruises. Since she was stupid enough to consider granting her sister's request, it couldn't be anywhere public in case Kristin decided to throw a tantrum. It wouldn't be above her. With the paparazzi on her tail looking for a shot of her phantom baby bump, locations were limited. Finally, Layla settled on a park near the elementary school they'd attended and texted her sister the time and location.

K. 10 AM SAT. THANK YOU!

It was a mistake and Layla knew it. She couldn't help herself. Joy was toxic and her parents had proven repeatedly that they'd do anything to protect their littlest girl, even to the extent of poisoning their other relationships. Layla understood in the theoretical sense but it broke her heart to see them sacrificing more of their family to Joy's disease. Kristin was caught in the middle. If she got free of her twin, she'd be alone without Layla. Alone sucked.

Layla wanted her whole family back but if all she got was one sister it was better than the solitude she had now. Maybe the two of them could rebuild what all of them had destroyed.

In the meantime, she'd just finished another up-close and personal, hands-on meeting with her ex-lover again and learned new and exciting ways to land on a marble floor.

Being an actress was so glamorous.

Martine Peeples was waiting for her as she limped to her trailer. "You're welcome to come in but I'm not talking until I choke down some Advil," Layla warned her.

The PR maven waited. She tucked her suited frame into a chair and sat patiently until Layla was ready for her. "Good news or bad news first?" Martine offered.

"Is there actually any good news or are you trying to break it to me gently?" Layla asked in reply.

Martine laughed. "No, there's actual good news. We've cleared up the 'you getting Russ fired' story. Put it to bed entirely."

"That's great. Thank you."

"Speaking of Russ, you two were concentrating pretty hard but did you notice Benny taking shots of your last rehearsal?"

"No." Layla ran the session back in her mind and couldn't picture the PR intern in the room. "He's getting a lot better at being discreet." Considering how the cast had almost mutinied the first time the young man had tried to organize a shoot, it was a huge improvement in a little over a month.

"It turns out he's a genius with a camera but only if the subjects don't know he's there. Anyway, as an FYI, you and Russ will be going up on the website for a behind the scenes bit for this episode."

"Fine." Layla snapped the word out before a yawn erupted. She barely managed to cover her mouth. "Sorry. That's fine about the pictures. If you send me the links, I'll put them out on my social media accounts."

Martine hesitated. "Benny said that you and Russ were working hard but that you were still getting tossed around a lot."

Layla shrugged. "It's a rough script. Hopefully the next one will be less physical." Then she realized what that comment was leading into. "I'm not pregnant! Honestly!"

"That's the bad news. We're still having trouble selling that story," Martine admitted.

"Baby bumps move papers," Layla agreed. "Even imaginary ones."

"Keep doing what you're doing. Hopefully these pictures can do double duty."

"Is there anything else I can do for the show?"

Martine made the strangest face. Layla had no idea what was going through the woman's head but it didn't seem to be a pissed-off expression. Considering how much damage control the woman had done after the fan appreciation contest, Layla didn't want to cause more work for her. "No," the woman drawled. "You've been great these last few weeks. Thank you. Keep it up and this will most likely blow over at the next news cycle."

A sigh escaped before she could stop it. Doing what she was doing was practically killing her. It still beat the alternative. Layla smiled gamely but she knew she wasn't fooling either of them. "Will do."

* * * *

Russ ached all over. Except his ass. That spot sent lightning bolts of pain right up his spine after Zeus accidentally dropped him on his arrow injury. Chris had been horrified at the slip. The concern was appreciated but it didn't help the pain.

He didn't want to imagine how badly Layla was hurting. Every stunt that he blocked, she had to perform and in this episode, they all ended up with her flat on her back. A year ago – hell, a month ago – she would have been bitching to beat the band but this past week, nothing. A couple groans when she'd landed hard but not a word of complaint. It hadn't gone unnoticed either.

Russ had thought on it and, aside from the first episode when Layla said she was still on probation, this season had been a complete turn-around of both her actions and her personality. She'd backtracked a couple times but never to the bitch-queen level of the last two. When she slipped, she'd apologized every time.

He thought for certain that after their break-up she'd fall back on old habits. She hadn't. If anything, she was trying even harder to climb out of the hole she'd dug for herself. He'd be really impressed if he didn't know the details about the hole.

The pain wasn't limited to his body. His brain hurt as well. Erin wasn't going crazy, not that he thought she was. Since she'd spoken to him, Russ had seen Jeremy Bowen around too. It was the craziest dance. Russ would spot him and try to get close, calling security if he had time. But the little rat was sneaky. Russ couldn't get close to him. Sometimes he thought he had the man cornered when Todd Olson would come at him from the opposite direction and the dealer would disappear somewhere in the middle.

He knew he spied Kristin hanging around Layla's trailer once. She'd spotted him and had hightailed it out of there immediately. At the time, Russ knew Layla to be filming so it wasn't like she was there to get more compromising photos. They still hadn't discovered the leak although the strategic pauses indicated they shared the same suspicion. Russ checked to make sure the new lock on the trailer door was still engaged and heard tires squealing in the parking lot before he made it that far.

Kristin was worrisome but the dealer was the bigger threat. At least the asshole was staying away from his girls. Right now he was an annoyance but a peripheral one. If he got close to anybody Russ cared about, the hunt would get a lot more personal.

Chapter 15

Green tea would have been a better choice, all soothing and caffeine-free and shit. Instead, Layla was sucking back a double espresso while she paced between the monkey bars and the swing set as she waited for Kristin, who was fifteen minutes late and counting.

She had no idea why she bothered to show up in the first place. Kristin was just as likely to show up as…shit, a Jackass movie had been nominated for an Oscar. The girl wasn't coming. Layla knew it.

So when her former assistant did show up, Layla was so shocked she squeezed her cardboard coffee cup so hard the lid popped off.

"I'm so, so sorry I'm late!" Kristin rushed. "I know you didn't want to meet with me in the first place and it looks like I stood you up. But I wanted to bring you coffee and the line was out of control." The twenty-year-old thrust a new cup at her. "Espresso, one sweetener."

She brought me lattes on the few times she bothered to bring me anything at all when she worked for me and now she gets my order right? This was definitely buttering up territory. Layla already knew she didn't want to hear what the favor was going to be. "Thanks."

"Can we sit?"

Layla brushed the leaves from the previous night's windstorm from the bench, then looked at her sister expectantly.

"Mom and Dad cut Joy off. Completely. They took back her car keys, her cell phone and her credit cards. They dropped her off at a treatment center and told her that if she didn't complete the month she wasn't getting any of them back." Kristin paused. "She slapped Mom. Mom slapped her back. That was how they left it."

"Is Mom okay?"

"Physically, she's fine. Emotionally…I think she's broken. She's been fighting against the idea of Joy being sick—"

"An alcoholic," Layla interrupted. "Joy has a disease but pretty words don't change what the result is."

"I know. Mom's been in denial for two years. Dad too. They can't pretend anymore."

Her little sister sounded old. And tired. Tired like she was, of the lies and the pretending and the effort it took to hide the truth from as many people as possible. "How are you doing?" Layla asked.

"I slept for the first time in a year last night knowing Joy wasn't going to call me to come get her from some bar or party or stranger's house." Tears started rolling down Kristin's cheeks but she didn't move to brush them away. "Yesterday I didn't have to arrange my day so that I was with her to make sure she wouldn't have time to start drinking. I didn't have to make plans to go with her to some place that didn't serve alcohol. I didn't have to sabotage her car or hide her keys. Do you know what a relief that is? And how horrible a sister I am to feel that way?"

There were no words. There was comfort. Layla pulled the sobbing girl into her arms and held tight. Layla had gone through the same breakthrough and breakdown when she'd opened her eyes to the reality of the situation.

Her coffee was long cold and she was out of napkins when Kristin was ready to move on. "I was a bad sister to Joy and a bad sister to you. I really liked working for you. It was a cool job. I wasn't trying to take advantage of you all the time but I kept putting covering for Joy in front of everything and everybody else."

There was resentment on Layla's part. Boatloads of

it. Intellectually she understood that her family wasn't trying to hurt her but that didn't negate the fact that they had. Layla didn't know if she had the energy to expand the new her to her personal life as well as her professional one but she wouldn't be able to live with herself if she didn't even try.

"So all the times you were late and left early?" Layla asked.

"Joy."

"The appointments and shopping dates?"

"Joy."

"And screwing up with Chris on the fan appreciation contest and then setting up the toga for Sydney when you knew she'd be afraid to show her scars?"

Kristin swallowed. "That was me. I tried to set it up so they had to call the next winner. Then she showed up anyway. At your job! After she sued you. I can't believe her. I didn't know what she was going to do so I tried to scare her off. You'd already paid enough for Sydney's accident…"

"You know that stunt not only cost you your job working for Chris but could have cost me mine." Although Layla wasn't as upset as she should have been. It was strange to think of Kristin as being somebody who had tried to have her back rather than somebody who was sticking knives into it.

"I fucked up."

"Yes, you did." Moving on. How could she hold a grudge when she'd done the same thing? "It's okay. You'll need to apologize to Chris and Sydney."

"What'll I say?"

"Try 'I'm sorry for messing up the phone calls and for the toga stunt.' You don't have to explain. Just apologize."

"Well, since I'm likely never going to see them again, that's not a problem."

"You'll see Chris on Monday. If you want your job back," Layla offered.

"Are you serious?"

"You are never late. You don't get time off for anything for at least three months. Definitely no vacation days. You keep your head down and your mouth shut until you've made all your apologies and I mean general apologies to everybody on set. I get your attitude. I taught you the attitude. But I was a queen bitch for almost two years and it's going to take me that long to earn back their respect. You were only a mini-bitch. You might have an easier road since you're starting earlier than I did."

"I can do that." Kristin laughed and checked her pockets. "Damn, I'm out of Kleenex."

"Me too."

Kristin looked around. "Don't tell Mom," she said before she wiped her nose on her sleeve.

"Ew!" Layla laughed.

"At least nobody got a picture of that."

Layla frowned. "Speaking of pictures, did you have anything to do with those shots of me puking?"

"How can you ask me that?"

"You were pissed when I fired you. You threatened me. You hadn't done that before."

"I can't believe you think I'd do that," Kristin repeated.

"Yes, you can. I'm sorry but I have to ask. Was it you?"

"No."

"You were there. Did you see anybody around who wasn't supposed to be there?" Layla pressed.

"Just security guys and crew. The same people as always."

"Crap. I wonder who it was?"

"I'll find out. I promise."

Layla slung her arm around her sister again. This hugging thing was getting to be a habit. "Don't worry about whoever it was. Just show up and do your job. That's all I need from you. Don't kid yourself. It's not going to be easy or fun. If you slip up I will let you know and you won't enjoy it." She squeezed hard for a second. "And talk to me about Joy. If she calls you for something. If you have bad dreams. Whatever. It's a shitty road to walk and you don't have to do it alone."

Kristin used her sleeve again. "What about Mom and Dad?"

"They aren't there yet." Layla let her sister go. "Go home. Sleep. Seven o'clock on Monday morning. I'll clear you on the gate. Don't be late. I'll have coffee in the trailer."

* * * *

Russ was drunk. Hammered. Fucking wasted.

Tom, his middle older brother handed him another beer anyway. Tom always did the unexpected, starting with his looks. Their paternal grandfather was Russian, and compared to the other three Vukovich boys, he was deathly pale. It seemed some of Grandpa's genes came out to play with him. Tom, unlike the others, always had a full supply of beer on hand, mostly because he preferred vodka. That wasn't a Russian thing, though; that was because of a misspent freshman year and too much Budweiser. Tom still couldn't drink the stuff. He said it was the smell.

"Woman problems?" he'd guessed when Russ showed up on Saturday afternoon.

Russ' grunt was his only response. Now he was ready to talk. The cool flow of air through the open garage door and the icy beer helped keep his temper under wraps.

"At first I thought she was just an ice-queen who looked hotter than fuck. I pushed through that and there was this whole other side, a nice one who was even hotter because she could be sweet and funny. Then I dug through that and found a cold-hearted bitch again and I do not like that bitch. But I think she only shows up when Layla needs somebody to deal with all the serious shit in her life because fuck knows that nobody has that girl's back." Even thinking about the dichotomy made him confused, which is what the beer was for.

"If she showed you her soft spot, why are you so pissed off? I thought you said she told you the truth?" Tom asked from his weight bench.

"First she lied to me. Why do all women lie to me, Tom? And then when she did tell me the truth, it sucked!"

"Dude, get a grip."

That wasn't helpful.

His brother continued. "Make a fucking decision. Either you want her to tell you the truth or you want her to lie. But stop punishing her because she did what you wanted. Man up."

Why the hell was this accountant he was related to arguing with logic? Russ didn't need to be told he was being an asshole and he sure didn't need to be told to stop acting like one. "So you think I should just wave my magic wand and pretend it's all okay?"

Tom puffed out a breath as he bench-pressed the barbell. "First of all, I don't want to know what she calls it. Second, don't wave it anywhere near me." He finished his set and paused for a minute. "Third, be damned sure you are pissed off at what she did and not the idea of what she did." He set the bar in the rack and sat up. "You're drunk, so pay attention. This is the important big brother stuff coming at you now. I don't know what Layla did. I do know that you weren't there. You don't get to judge decisions that were made in the heat of the moment. You've been in firefights. You know that you make choices at the time and have to live with them. You've got to remember that. And in the end she did tell you the truth."

Russ nodded his very heavy head. His brother was right about that. He was going to give that some serious thought. After his next beer.

"Fuck it, you're not going to remember. Go inside and crash on the couch. I'll drive you to Leo's tomorrow for breakfast and remind you then. Then I'll make you both sorry for the beer when I tell you what's wrong with your books. In detail."

Chapter 16

It wasn't like she was eavesdropping on purpose. Layla had to tie her sneaker before heading in to see Erin and she stopped under the window. She wasn't the one who opened it.

"I'm telling you it's pod people. They've got her whole family!" Erin argued.

"You can't know that," Russ said.

"Oh no? Kristin Aquino was just in here apologizing to me. Don't get me wrong, I love the new Layla but they are all starting to freak me out."

She wasn't going to get a better opening than that. Layla knocked on the door before she opened it. "Good morning!" she called brightly. Okay, it was a bit wicked but she smiled when they both jumped. Especially Russ.

She'd received another Hera-hating script but it wasn't as bad as the previous one. She wasn't in it much since hers was the secondary storyline. Normally she'd be upset at the lack of screen time but frankly she could use the break to let last week's bruises fade.

"Did you know that Kristin was back?" Russ asked.

"Yes. We had a talk. She's here on probation. Please let me know if she is anything but completely professional," Layla asked.

"Why the change of heart?" Russ pressed.

He didn't deserve an answer. She gave him one anyway. "Kristin fucked up. She also made a tough decision and is working her way back from it. I think everybody deserves a second chance."

She stared him down as he said good-bye to Erin. Once he was gone, she took a seat in the styling chair. "I mean it. If Kristin steps out of line, you need to tell me. You suffered enough with me. You don't need a mini-me running around."

"You are such a little thing I don't think there could be a mini version."

Layla caught Erin's eyes in the mirror. "I'm serious. I was a bitch and I'm sorry. It won't happen again."

"I'm getting that. On a different subject entirely, ask me what Russ was doing in here."

Ruing the fact that he was stupid enough to dump me? Not likely. Stubborn ass. "What was Russ doing in here?"

"Dickhead Jeremy update. I thought I'd been seeing him around. I had. Russ was warning me to be careful until they figure out why he keeps coming back here. He hasn't tried to see me. How about you?"

"Nothing. But the fact that he's here can't be good."

"I know."

The news ate at Layla all day to the extent that she texted Kristin to tell her to work in her trailer and keep the door locked. Even working with Caitlin wasn't enough to distract the worry.

The new girl was good. She'd been cast in a three-episode arc to play Psyche, the mortal that Eros fell in love with until she was banished by Aphrodite. If the character was popular, Caitlin Kelly could become a regular. When Layla saw her chemistry with Sean, she was ready to put money on the pair becoming an item before her first episode was even finished shooting. Layla had almost as much fun watching the pair flirt on set as she did watching Sean strike out repeatedly when the cameras stopped rolling.

The timing of her casting was suspect. The show's star began dating a woman who had a friend that was an unknown actress and now said unknown actress was here. It was beyond Layla's control but she was thankful the woman had a decent amount of talent. Everybody needed a break; if Sydney gave Caitlin hers, more power to Caitlin for making it work.

The only upside of the script was that it didn't call for any time with Russ. It had taken everything she had to keep it together for all of their scenes last week. It didn't help that every time she looked at him, she pictured him without his clothes. She knew every inch of him now. The secret crush was easier.

Sometimes Layla hated being right. She was walking Erin to her car when she got a panicked call.

"Layla, can you come to your trailer? Like right the fuck now? I don't know what to do," Kristin asked all in one breath.

"Is Jeremy there?"

"No. Not exactly."

Erin and her bat ears veered away from her car and hooked her arm around Layla's. "That doesn't sound good. I'm sorry you ever got involved with that dickhead."

So was Layla.

* * * *

Russ did not expect to find Kristin alone in Layla's trailer when he got the call from Erin. Despite the stylist's warning, he really didn't expect the apology.

"I'm sorry we ruined your date," Layla's little sister said. "I should have been watching Joy closer. She's in treatment now."

"That sounds like a good thing."

"I know you're not seeing my sister anymore." Kristin glanced through the screen door, and then continued. "Layla wasn't supposed to tell anybody what happened but she would have trusted you enough to explain. It wasn't her fault. We made her take that plea.

We begged her. And worse."

"It was her choice."

"Then you're a better person than all of us. Do the wrong thing or your whole family is going to turn their backs on you? I wouldn't have been that strong either. I'm lucky she's trying to forgive me. With what we did, I don't know if she'll ever be able to forgive my parents or Joy." She suddenly popped to her feet, smiling brightly. "Coke?" she asked out of nowhere.

He didn't understand where the subject change came from until the latch on the screen door clicked and his dream woman walked in, looking not at all dreamy. She was too pale, too stressed, too jittery. He'd forgotten that this was her safe place where she could let the mask slip. Layla had seemed fine but in the presence of people she trusted – Erin and Kristin – she let the worry show. Then she spotted him in the corner and blinked, erasing the stress on her face and replacing it with the same smile he'd been getting all week. She was a hell of an actress; till that moment he'd thought it was real.

"Russ?"

It was a polite but confused greeting. Any hopes she'd arranged this meeting vanished. "Kristin called me," he explained.

"And you came?"

Now that was insulting. "She knew I called security the first time Bowen came around. She asked who she should call to follow up."

"I'm sure it's fine. I'm sorry to have bothered you."

"I'm not," Kristin interrupted. "I think we need help with this." Then she told them why.

God, they needed more help than he could provide. They needed so much Russ called Leo to get him involved. What a cluster-fuck, and Russ was only on the periphery. Somehow Jeremy had made it past the doorman in Layla's apartment but had been stopped at the elevator. The building's security company had emailed a photo of the intruder which had prompted Kristin's actions.

Statistically speaking, Bowen should have gone away. The fact that he'd fixated on Layla was not good. He'd moved beyond annoyance to full-out threat.

But that wasn't Russ' problem. He knew he'd pulled himself out of any position to help Layla. It was getting harder to stick to his decision. His original feelings hadn't changed; Layla was wrong to have remained silent. Lying was the one thing he couldn't handle. It was his hard line on the subject he was beginning to regret. Nothing could undo what happened to Sydney, and Layla had paid for her silence. Was he certain that Joy would have gotten a different sentence? No. Tom was right; he hadn't been there. He didn't pretend he was perfect. Why did he expect Layla to be?

The results of the meeting were less than he hoped for but probably still more than he deserved.

"I'll send Leo over tomorrow to scope out what he needs to do for security at your place," he confirmed.

"Thanks. Kristin will meet him tomorrow in the lobby."

"Okay."

It was a win-win situation for everybody. Leo got his first big-name client for Pacific Personal Security, Layla got the protection she needed, and Russ didn't have to spend time with the woman he'd dumped.

So why did it feel like he'd lost big time?

Chapter 17

Another week, another calamity in the exciting life and loves of Layla 'Hera' Andrews. She should get that printed on a t-shirt. For everything that went right, something bigger went horribly, horribly wrong.

She had two things go right this week, which was pretty much a record in her recent history. Kristin was working out. Her sister was working, period. All the crap she was supposed to handle the first time around that Layla had been stuck with was now off Layla's plate. She now had spare time. It was a novel concept. She spent most of it with Kristin and Erin, so it was almost like being at work only she was having a good time.

Even work was enjoyable this week. They had a phenomenal script, one of the ones that made a season worthwhile. Hera was in the secondary storyline again but Layla didn't care because the episode was that good. The entire cast was energized. Olympus was the place to be this week.

So, of course, the rest of her life had to go down the toilet.

Joy found a phone and called Kristin in the middle of the night, begging her twin to come pick her up. When Kristin refused, Joy turned on her like a rabid dog, calling her every vile name under the sun. Detox was a bitch. Kristin hung up on her baby sister and immediately called her older one, which was a good decision. Layla would have liked the decision better if it hadn't been made at two in the morning but she eventually got Kristin calmed down and managed to get another ninety minutes of sleep before getting up for an early start the next day on set.

Russ was still avoiding her on set. Layla was almost in tears. She didn't know what else she could do. The big jerk had made it clear that he didn't want to see her again unless it was absolutely professionally necessary. He was acting as if they'd never happened at all. It was like he had no clue what coming face-to-face with him every day did to her. Or maybe he did but he didn't care.

It would be easier to believe the second. It would give her a reason to hate him. She wanted to. Anything would be better than this combination of grief and understanding of his actions. Layla felt like a brokenhearted love song. She knew what Russ was doing was right for him. The fact that it was wrong for her was something she was willing to live with because she wanted him to be happy, even if it wasn't with her. Love was brutal. Unfortunately, as bad as that was, it was only number two on her list of ways her life sucked.

Number one was Dickhead Jeremy. With a bullet. Layla would have said that out loud but the cops in her trailer might have taken it the wrong way, especially with the news they brought. Somebody had beaten the hell out of Jeremy Bowen. He said it was her.

Not her, personally. Nobody on the planet would believe that she was capable of doing what the pictures in front of her showed. The dickhead was claiming she hired somebody to rough him up.

It was a good idea. She wished she'd thought of it. Layla was careful not to say that out loud either.

This was going to end up as nothing more than a waste of everybody's time but there was no way she could avoid it. Layla agreed to go down to the station to give her statement.

She didn't agree to Kristin's suggested escort. "No," Layla insisted.

"But Laylay," Kristin protested.

"No, you will absolutely not call Russ. I'm not some

helpless little princess who needs him to swoop in and rescue me. I'm the Queen of Olympus. I've got this."

Kristin looked unconvinced.

"I'm also not a complete moron. Call Dad. I'm going to need a lawyer to watch my back."

* * * *

The offices of Pacific Personal Security looked different somehow. More real, less fake. Two years around television sets provided Russ with a good reality meter. The rooms and desks were dirtier and more disorganized and less perfect than they had been a week ago. It was better.

Being hailed as a hero didn't hurt either. Kristin, and by proxy Layla, had taken Leo's security review to heart to the tune of a whole new system with all the bells and whistles for her apartment as well as a companion system for her car. It was a nice chunk of change. Kristin had even provided a testimonial using Layla's name and permission.

To celebrate such a score, there was beer.

But first, there was paperwork.

Permits and police checks and insurance forms and employment papers. In triplicate. Russ took a moment to mourn the tree that had sacrificed itself for his new job. He tried not to think of the one document he'd been avoiding. He still needed to write his letter of resignation.

That was going to be hard. He liked the people on Olympus. He liked his bosses and God knew he owed them for hiring him when he was looking for work after he'd been released from the service. It had been an excellent transitioning job but it wasn't what he wanted to do for the rest of his life. Some of the stunt and fight coordinators he worked with were gunning for a career in movies. Russ was putting in time and he knew it. Getting out was a good thing for him and for the guy replacing him who would be excited to go to work every morning. Russ needed a double alarm to get out of bed.

The only days he was up early were the ones he knew he'd be working with Layla. Those were the extra careful shaving, a little extra cologne days. Thank God for her sister because if Kristin hadn't called, Russ wouldn't have seen Layla at all in the last couple weeks.

Now that he was in the office, he could catch up on her. Leo had files.

Russ excused himself from the party and wandered towards the head. Then he passed the bathroom door and ducked into Leo's office, which for now was doubling as the file room.

The filing cabinet was locked and Leo's computer was password protected.

L-A-D-I-E-S-M-A-N-2-1-7 was a no-go.

M-E-T-A-L-L-I-C-A-2-1 was strike two even though it combined two of his brother's obsessions – his favorite band and Deion Sanders in his wonder years.

A third try would have locked him out of the system but he got busted first.

"Whatcha lookin' for, baby brother?"

Russ slammed the lid of the laptop closed. "Score on the…" Nobody was playing anything at four o'clock on a Wednesday afternoon.

"The score on Layla's file? You aren't getting close to that one. Personal involvement with clients is strictly forbidden, not to mention a disastrously bad idea when it comes to maintaining professional judgment."

"Just tell me what's happening with her."

"She's fine. You should be keeping your distance. You made it clear to her that you were through. If mom found out you were stringing this piece of tail along she'd smack you."

"Layla's not a piece!"

"Let's see. You've been raving for years about how hot she is even while you were complaining about how much of a bitch she was. Then you finally date her and, presumably with the whole walking-into-walls, compulsive-phone-checking sex-face impression, get some. Then the first chance you get, you say she did something to piss you off and you dump her. That's pretty much the definition of a piece." Leo held up his hand to shut Russ up. "Look, you know the highlights. We're trying to keep tabs on Bowen but he's a slick little fuck. Layla, on the other hand, is cooperating. She's as protected as we can make her. Move on."

Russ was gearing up to argue again when his phone went off. It was Kristin and her news pissed him off.

"I know what Bowen was doing when he disappeared," Russ informed Leo.

"Do tell."

"He was getting the shit beat out of him. He's filed charges against Layla. She's being questioned right now."

"I thought you were kidding when you said life conspired to make her so mean. Nobody's luck is that bad."

Chapter 18

It was nowhere near as fun and exciting as it looked on television. The tiny little interview room was filled to overflowing with three chairs, a table, two cops, Layla, and her lawyer. The blank, bland walls and plain furniture were not conductive to a 'let's chat' atmosphere, but then, they weren't supposed to be. The setting was all about intimidation and scaring confessions loose. Since Layla was innocent, she couldn't give them one, and since her lawyer was present, she couldn't tell them that anyway. She kept her mouth shut and let her representative do the talking.

Blaine Colfer was an associate in the criminal division of Layla's step-father's firm. The man was only four inches taller than she was, which put him at 5'3" and left him the second shortest person in the room. What he lacked in height, he made up for in tenacity. Layla didn't think she spoke more than half a dozen sentences in the entire hour the investigating officers questioned her about the attack on Jeremy Bowen.

"This is a joke," Colfer repeated to her on their way out. "It's a nuisance charge. Youe alibi is solid and there's nothing to indicate you had anything to do with Bowen's beating. If anything more comes of this, I'll be shocked. I don't think he'll be dumb enough to try anything else."

"Never underestimate the power of stupid," Layla warned him.

He schooled his face into a serious legal business look. "This reeks of desperation for Bowen. Both he and the cops know they should be looking at his drug connections. He should be worried about them, not fixating on you. Be careful till he's caught."

Layla nodded towards the waiting area where both Leo and Russ Vukovich stood leaning against the wall, waiting. "After Dickhead Jeremy tried to get into my apartment, I hired security."

"Good. Keep them close," Colfer advised.

Her father's employee or not, Layla was glad he didn't hang around with what he charged per hour. It was bad enough she was going to have to pay for travel time during rush hour. After Colfer left, Layla walked over to Leo and Russ.

"Do you need a ride home?" Leo asked.

"No, I drove my car."

"I'll follow you home," Leo offered.

"No, I will," Russ interrupted.

"It's not necessary," Layla protested.

"I want to," Russ said.

Layla turned to Leo. "Can you give us a minute?" When he nodded and stepped away, she took a breath and held it for a ten count. "Why are you doing this, Russ?"

"Doing what?"

"Do you know how hard it is for me to see you?" Layla whispered. "To look at you and remember the two best weeks I've ever had in my life and then have to remind myself it's gone every time you smile at me? And for what? Because I made a mistake before I met you? Do you know how much that hurts?"

Russ's jaw dropped. "Layla, I never meant to hurt you."

"You did a shitty job. I don't want to be blunt but I will. I don't want you to follow me home. You shouldn't have come down to check on me, especially since your brother did too and I'm paying for that service. Go home, Russ."

"We're not dating anymore but can't we still be friends?"

Could she? Could she settle for crumbs after having all of him? Layla knew she was already heavy on enemies and light on allies. She ought to settle for the friendship offered but she wasn't certain it was really friendship when all she'd get out of it was pain and regret.

Layla already missed him to the point her heart actually ached. When she closed her eyes, she couldn't feel his arms around her any more. She'd hidden the coffee in her kitchen and had switched to tea, the memories of Russ' reaction to her stash now more painful than funny. Every day she saw him by accident was too damned hard. She wasn't tough enough to do it on purpose.

Layla had stopped lying to herself a long time ago. Russ said he didn't want the lies either. "No, I don't think we can. We can be colleagues till you start your new job but I think it's best if we keep it professional."

He looked stunned that she'd turned him down and she didn't understand why. It was his idea.

* * * *

Fuck that shit.

Yeah, he'd been upset and he'd said some stuff. She'd shocked the hell out of him when she spilled everything in the truck that afternoon. He was going to react. What kind of woman listened to a man when he spouted off crap like that though? She didn't even fight for him. He was ready to forgive her for what she'd done because he wanted her back so bad.

Didn't she realize how good they'd been together? He wasn't just talking emotionally either, although – fight aside – that had been really good too. He missed her physically. Years of fantasies didn't compare to days of the real thing. He'd even gone out and bought a bottle of her shampoo and conditioner to keep in his shower. That crap was expensive but it at least smelled like her. His new electric blanket couldn't replace the warmth she put out under the covers though, or the soft touch when she'd snuggle up against his arm in her sleep.

Despite what she'd said at the police station, Layla wasn't the only one who'd fallen hard. He didn't understand it but the actress fit his life perfectly. He was no relationship guru but he knew good when he had it.

Damn it, she needed to accept his apology and get over him being a jerk already.

Although he had been a pretty big jerk. Plus, she had other stuff on her mind, like being stalked by a drug dealer. That wasn't helping his game at all. It was, however, something he could help with. All he had to do now was convince his brother to put him on the case.

Fuck Leo too, because he wasn't listening either. "I'm not asking to be assigned to Layla's security detail but I can track this little shit down."

"And then do what?" Leo asked. "The guy isn't under arrest. He's out on bail. Unless he's doing something illegal, we can't do anything."

"He's harassing Layla."

"Yes, but it's not the illegal kind of harassment which sucks for her. We also can't encourage him to stop because he's already eliminated that option with the counter-harassment suit. That was pretty smart for a guy like him."

Leo's gaze drifted to the window as he considered his last sentence. His big brother had a point. The dickhead wasn't bright enough to come up with that move on his own. "Don't cut me out, Leo. I don't want to fuck things up with Layla again. This guy is bad news."

"You said that you've been hanging out with her at work. Keep doing that. It's all any of us can do for now and since people are used to seeing you around anyway they won't think anything of it."

Russ swallowed hard. "I can't."

"Why not?"

"She doesn't want me anywhere near her."

"Talk to her. Explain."

"I don't think it will matter."

"Make it matter. You're all we've got until we can get some more men on the job. We need to be close and we're out of options."

Maybe not.

Chapter 19

The last day of a fantastic script generated mixed feelings. It was good to work on something so enjoyable but it sucked knowing it was coming to an end. Layla doubted she'd have another one as good this season. She didn't want it to be over but the weekend and some sleep would be an acceptable finale.

Kristin had spent the last couple nights on the sofa for good cause. Joy was nothing if not persistent. She'd tracked down Kristin's new phone number and was working her twin for all she was worth. Personally, Layla suspected her parents of passing along her digits but she wasn't going to voice that idea to her little sister. Kristin was still struggling with the idea that she'd been enabling Joy for the last year. Finding out their parents still were wouldn't help her.

It wasn't like Layla was sleeping anyway. The few times she drifted off she dreamed of Russ. She had some over-the-counter sleeping pills but she refused to take them while she was working. One tonight would knock her out well into Saturday morning. So there was good reason for Erin to repeat herself while Layla was in the chair.

"Layla, are you listening to me?" the stylist asked.

"Sorry. What?"

"I said that Russ called to say he'd be by this morning with his brothers to show them around. You know you're welcome to hang out here but if you want to avoid him, you're better off waiting someplace else."

"Thanks."

Erin's support of the Russ situation meant the world to Layla. The stylist liked them together; she'd said so repeatedly. But when the chips were down and being in the unusual position of being able to hear both sides of the story, Erin had cast herself on Layla's side. She didn't mention anything but Layla suspected Erin's history with Jeremy Bowen was coloring her decision a little bit.

Layla took the warning in the spirit it was meant and disappeared to a corner of the soundstage where she could watch a scene being set up. She hadn't heard anyone come in behind her until a young voice said, "Hi, Miss Andrews."

Perhaps she was a little more on edge than she thought. Quiet Benny Duarte should not have caused a squeal like the one she let loose. "Sorry, Benny. Can I help you?"

"No, I need more shots for the website. Ms. Peeples said she likes me working from behind the scenes," he said. He was only about ten years younger than her but Layla thought of him as a kid. It was the face. He was going to be carded until he was well into his thirties.

"Yeah, she told me you killed at the background shots."

"She did?" A broad smile split his face, his brown eyes disappearing into slits. He rubbed his shaved head as he fought his goofy grin. "I should probably get back to work then."

He'd barely disappeared when Sean took his spot. "I need a favor," he said. "Actually, I need two."

This was a first. Not an unwelcome first but still. "Shoot."

"Can you show me that mark thing one more time? I'm starting to look again," he said.

"No problem." It wasn't. It was even kind of flattering. It took a lot of practice and training to be able to stop at a predetermined "mark", in most cases an "X" taped to the floor, without looking for it. Layla got the feeling that nobody had spent much time teaching Sean the technique, although he picked it up quickly. He seemed to have a better sense of spatial orientation than a lot of people. She assumed it was because he was used to keeping track of where his teammates were on the court. "What's the second thing?"

"What's wrong with women?"

"Men," Layla answered promptly.

Sean erupted into laughter, startling some of the nearby P.A.s. "Fair enough. What's wrong with a woman when you ask her out on a date and she smirks at you and says she has to go to work and walks away giggling?"

Holy crap, this was the good gossip straight from the source. Layla even knew who he was referring to. "I'd guess that the woman suspected your version of a date and hers were substantially different. Or your version of asking. Or both," she said. "Caitlin turn you down?"

"Flat," Sean confirmed. "How did you know it was her? Did she say something?"

"You know that Caitlin is friends with Sydney who is going out with Chris, right?"

"Yeah."

"You know that Chris and everyone else on the set is well aware of your reputation as a ladies' man, right?" she continued.

"I haven't tried to hide it."

Layla dropped her sarcastic tone for a moment. "Which is great. Really. You're an upfront guy and as a woman, I appreciate that. But if Caitlin isn't interested in a fling, there's not a whole lot you can do to change her mind."

"There's nothing wrong with casual." A hint of defensiveness leaked into his voice.

"There's nothing wrong with slow and monogamous

and long-term either. You're just not going to find a lot of people who are willing to be both. It's like sushi. You either like it or you don't. There's no wrong answer but there's no middle ground either."

Sean stood silently for a moment. "That sucks. It's true but it sucks."

"So many things do."

"She's really hot."

"Yes, she is." Layla had learned while chatting with Caitlin between takes that the new actress's looks came from a Cuban-Irish heritage. The new woman pulled the best from both sides of her family. "There is one other possibility."

"Oh?" When his eyebrows met his hairline Layla knew he suffered from the real thing. Nothing else would generate such hopefulness.

"Maybe she really does have another job. This is three episodes for her, not a full season. A girl needs to eat."

"You think?"

"You'd have to ask her. Want to meet tomorrow to do the mark thing?"

"Yeah, thanks. I appreciate you not saying anything to the guys. I get enough crap from them."

"No problem."

Sean wandered off to wherever he'd come from. Layla scanned the area to make sure that Russ and his brothers hadn't snuck in while she was distracted but had to stop halfway through her search when her phone rang. She glanced at the call display. "Hey, Erin, what's up?"

"I need help."

Layla grinned. "Hit me, I'm on a roll."

"I need you to find Russ."

She hit the brakes. "Excuse me?"

"Look, I was out and I swung by the...never mind. Dickhead Jeremy is here."

"What? Did you call security?"

"No."

"Then call security!" Layla shouted.

"I can't. Todd Olson was the guy who met him at the gate. Layla, I'm pretty sure I saw a gun."

"You probably did. Olson carries one."

"No, I think Jeremy has one."

Of course he did. Honest to God, how could one person's life be this fucked up? "Where are you now?"

"Hauling ass back to the hair and make-up trailer."

"When you get there, lock yourself in. Understand?"

She barely waited for an answer before ending the call and dialing Russ' number from memory since she'd deleted it from her contacts. Layla dodged around scaffolding and over cables on the floor. She couldn't believe it. Whose luck was this bad? She snorted. Besides hers.

The expanse between the building and trailers was eerily deserted as most of the crew and cast prepared for an upcoming shot. There were only two people in sight. One of whom was the last person on earth she wanted to see.

Paranoid beyond belief, Layla tried to watch every open spot around her as she approached Sydney and Chris. "You can't be here," she said to the woman.

"Always a pleasure to see you again too, Layla."

"Listen to me. Has Chris told you anything about the shit going on with me and a dealer they busted here a while back?"

The anger on Sydney's face morphed to wariness. "He said the guy attacked you in your trailer."

"He did. Now he's back. With a gun." Layla tugged

on Sydney's arm to pull her out of the potential line of fire but the other woman wouldn't move. Chris grabbed Sydney's other arm and held her fast.

"So call security," he snapped.

"Security is part of the problem. Get to your trailer and lock yourself in, okay?"

"What are you talking about? How can security be part of the problem?" Sydney asked.

Why was she wasting time arguing? "Look, I'm trying to help you. You've already suffered burn scars. I'd really rather not add bullet holes to the list of Layla-induced damage. Get gone! Chris, get her out of here!"

Layla spent precious seconds making sure that Sydney and Chris did indeed get inside the trailer while she redialed Russ's number. He wasn't answering. If he was blocking her number, she was going to be pissed. She stopped to scroll through her list until Leo's name came up. She'd forgotten she'd filed it under Pacific Personal Security and not Vukovich.

At least Leo answered. "Layla, is something wrong?"

"Yeah. Jeremy Bowen is here somewhere and according to Erin it was Todd Olson who signed him through the gate. She thinks she saw Bowen holding a gun. I have concerns." Layla heard a familiar metallic thump as she approached her trailer. It was the same sound Jeremy had made when he tried to kick his way in last time. "Shit, they're trying to get into my trailer! I just had that door repaired!"

Footsteps hitting concrete echoed through the line. "We're at the commissary. That's not even half a mile away. Lock yourself in the bathroom. Go out the window if you have to. We're coming."

"I'm not in my trailer. Kristin is."

"Hide."

"I'm not letting them get my sister!"

A new voice came over the line. "Layla, run. We'll be there before they get inside." Russ was using his deep commanding voice, which she would have happily obeyed if her sister's life weren't on the line.

"You're at the freaking commissary! I'll draw them off."

"Jesus, she thinks she's Rambo," Leo said. Apparently they had her on speaker.

On the plus side, she knew the area. On the downside, so did Todd. If she hid and they found her she'd be screwed. If she did nothing her sister would be.

Help was coming. The commissary was a three minute flat out run. If she went that way, all she'd have to do was keep ahead of Bowen and Olson.

"Russ, I'm coming to you."

"Layla, no!"

"I'm out of options." It was mostly true. She had other choices but she wasn't willing to put anyone at risk to cover her ass.

Layla strutted up to the end of her trailer. The dickhead was standing lookout while Todd was crouched by the door, flipping through his key ring. "Are you gentlemen looking for me?"

There was a split second when they looked confused. Then they looked pissed. Layla took off, her sneakers spitting up gravel as she tried to find traction. "Incoming!" she yelled, hoping the warning would be understandable as her arms pumped, carrying her phone away from her mouth.

She lost time taking the first corner wide but it was worth it. The wardrobe rack that rolled forward almost clotheslined Olson and Bowen. She heard cursing when they scrambled around it. Fuck, those soundstages were huge, she thought as she started to gasp as she passed the second one. Layla turned at the third one and cut between two garbage bins as she headed for the main thoroughfare. She burst through and saw she'd ended up behind all the Vukovich boys.

"Hey!" she shouted.

They skidded to a stop and she pointed behind her into the alley between the buildings.

Russ pointed towards the open-air commissary. "Go!" Then he led his brothers into the shadows.

Chapter 20

Dear God, for once let her listen. Don't let her argue or come back to check on us. Russ burst into through the narrow opening and saw Olson and Bowen coming at him hard. Todd slowed down when he saw him. Bowen showed no sign of recognition and came at him full speed. Good. Russ was looking for a fight.

Leo went straight for Olson. Russ watched for long enough to see that the twenty-year LAPD veteran wasn't going to have any problem with an out of shape twenty-something rent-a-cop.

Tom, he was pleased to note, backed his ass up against the side of the soundstage wall and stayed out of the way.

And that left Jeremy for him. Mindful of Layla's warning that the drug dealer might have a gun, Russ made sure the man's hands were empty when he rushed him. He rammed Bowen into the nearest garbage bin and heard something crack that wasn't him.

"You fucker!" Bowen screamed. He reached into his jacket and Russ jumped him again, grappling with his hands. Fortunately he had size, leverage and training on his side. He battered Bowen's hands against the heavy metal bin until the other guy dropped the gun. Russ kicked it away and shoved, hard.

It turned out that Bowen was a dirty street brawler. A good one. Russ preferred a more civilized beating, in a ring with gloves and rules and shit. But he was willing to make the exception in this case. The men traded punches that rocked both of them. Bowen tended to aim for his head with jabs which weren't too hard to block. When Russ returned the blows, he went for the torso since the dickhead left himself open.

"Who are you?" Bowen gasped between punches.

"I'm the guy who's going to make sure you never get anywhere near Layla again."

The threat probably would have been more effective if the guy hadn't switched it up and landed a blow to his gut. Bowen was more agile in the fight than Russ had anticipated, especially considering that he'd been tossed over a stair railing and beat up a second time not too long ago. Then Russ realized his attacker was at full strength when he assaulted Layla and that really pissed him off. Layla could have easily ended up in the hospital, or worse, if Russ hadn't arrived when he did.

Anger was a great motivator. The adrenaline spike was what he needed. He let loose a combination that quickly put Bowen on the ground, groaning, one hand wrapped around his knee, the other cupping his nuts.

The gun shot had Russ dropping down right beside him.

He lifted his head and saw...he didn't understand what he was seeing. Leo was on the ground. Todd Olson was on his knees with his arms in the air, and Tom of all people was standing in front of him pointing Leo's pistol at his head. Of all the people in the alley, the accountant was the last one who should be holding a weapon.

Russ popped to his feet and approached his brother from the side. "Hey, Tom, you okay?" he asked, his voice even, hoping not to startle him.

"I'm fine, Russ. You want to take this maybe?"

"That'd be good." Russ slipped his hands over his brother's and took over aiming the gun. Tom stepped back and helped Leo to his feet.

The tableau froze again. Todd was too smart to get up with a gun trained on him and Bowen wasn't going anywhere. Leo rested against Tom's side, his balance still not right.

"We need to get something straight before the cops get here. Layla called us for help and we met her at the end of the alley."

Russ nodded. Leo must have gotten his bell rung pretty hard if he was uncertain of the events of the last couple minutes.

"Then we saw these guys coming and subdued them."

"Yeah, man," Russ agreed. "Are you sure you're okay?"

"Yes. We subdued them and then I fired a warning shot but Olson jumped me and I dropped my gun. You ended up with it, Russ."

"Tom picked it up," Russ corrected. "He fired it."

"No, I did," Leo insisted.

"How hard did you hit your head?" Russ asked. "You had your hands full with Olson."

Leo swore. "Shut up, Russell and think. It's my gun. I, a licensed private investigator, fired it. You, also licensed, have it now. Tom, our brother who we both know is a great shot but who is not licensed, was nowhere near a weapon that could end up having charges against these two thrown out of court and back on the street to try again."

"But Tom fired it. We all know it," Russ protested.

"Did you see him fire it?" Leo asked.

"Yes, it was him."

"I didn't ask if it was him. I asked if you saw him pull the trigger," Leo persisted. "Because I'm pretty sure all your attention was on taking down Bowen way over there down the alley."

"Okay, so I didn't see him—"

"So are you calling me a liar with no proof?" Leo

interrupted again.

"Leo, what are you doing?"

"I'm protecting you and Tom and your girlfriend. Don't fuck this up, Russell."

"You want me to lie to the cops?" No. Hell, no.

"You work for me. So does Tom. I'm responsible for my employee's actions and that's what I'm doing. I'm taking responsibility. Are you telling me that one of your commanding officers never stepped up when you'd done something wrong under their watch?"

"That's different."

"How?"

Russ didn't know but it was. "I will not lie."

"You do understand the situation, don't you?"

"I won't lie."

"Fine. But be fucking sure that you tell the truth and nothing but. You fought with Bowen, you heard a shot and you saw Tom standing there holding the gun. That is all you know. Do not volunteer your thoughts, opinions or theories, Russell." Leo plucked the weapon from Russ's hands and stuffed it back into his holster.

Russ opened his mouth to argue when he realized why the gun was out of sight. LAPD cars blocked off the end of the alley and uniformed patrolmen rushed to the scene. Layla had apparently hit the commissary and dialed 911, bypassing studio security since she had no idea who else might be involved. That was sound thinking. His girl knew how to keep her cool.

He tried to spot her. More cops gathered. More security, more gawkers. Ambulances. She could have been hidden behind people in the crowd but he thought she would have worked her way forward to the crime scene tape. If nothing else, he expected her to check if they had survived the gunshot.

She wasn't there. Anywhere.

Jesus, they'd risked their lives for her. This was a hell of a thank you. His family...

Right. Her family. She'd probably gone to check on Kristin. Russ still couldn't believe that Layla had taken on both Olson and Bowen to protect her younger sister. Yes, she'd done more for Joy but that had been accidental, at least at first. This time she stuck her neck way the hell out there deliberately.

Russ shook his head. Speaking of sticking necks out. Leo was taking a hell of a risk. The cops likely wouldn't question their statements too much. All three of them had handled the gun, therefore all three of them would test positive for gunshot residue. Bowen had still been down for the count when the cops showed up, so he wouldn't be able to say anything either way. Technically Russ couldn't either—he hadn't seen the gun being discharged.

He understood where Leo was coming from. Tom was a fucking accountant. The only reason he was on set in the first place was so Russ could show off a little to his older brother about how cool his job was. The Vukovich boys may have grown up in Los Angeles but growing up they had nothing to do with anybody in the entertainment industry. Tom had been suitably impressed with the tour; he'd straight out admitted that he'd been a little star-struck meeting some of Russ's friends. He didn't need to get pulled into this mess, and it was going to get messy.

But lie? Tom would be in serious trouble. Bowen and Olson could walk. If they did, those two would fuck up again and Russ and Leo would be on hand to get them before they got anywhere near Layla again. Tom, on the other hand, would not come out clean.

What exactly was the lie? He hadn't seen Tom pull the trigger. He knew but he couldn't prove it. Leo was taking responsibility for what had happened with his gun. Nobody died. All Russ had to do was not volunteer information.

Tom was shaky when they got into the back of the cruiser. Russ kept one hand on his shoulder, trying not to flinch when tremors racked his brother. "Don't worry, Tommy, you're okay. Your family has your back."

They were halfway to the station when Russ realized that he'd made his decision. And what a hypocrite it made him.

Layla was right. She always had been.

Chapter 21

Kristin was fully tucked into Layla's monster-sized bed, under a stack of lightweight blankets and wrapped around a green stuffed pig Layla had won at a fair at some point in junior high. Layla had panicked when she'd raced back to her trailer to find the door jammed into the frame. She hadn't been able to pull it open. Kristin hadn't been able to kick it loose from the inside either. Instead her little sister popped the screen from the bedroom window and wormed her way out, Layla holding her legs and trying to ease her drop to the concrete.

Blaine Colfer made another trip from the office to the police station. The man was earning his paycheck this month. Fortunately, Layla and Kristin were called for witness statements only. Layla told Colfer to stay with Erin as well, and to send the bills for representing all three of them to her. Considering how much they hadn't seen, the three of them were done relatively quickly.

"No, I didn't know that" was Layla's most constant refrain when the police questioned her about Todd Olson, the security guard. No, she didn't know that Jeremy Bowen was friends with said guard. No, she didn't know that Olson was the conduit that set up the introduction between the supplier and his customers at the studio.

Once she was filled in on those facts, it was an easy deduction to realize Olson was the person who leaked the photos of her to the press. She never considered him as a possibility; even more than the crew, his uniform allowed him to slip into the background to be overlooked and forgotten. Kristin bit her tongue trying to swallow the "I told you so" but Layla could tell she was pleased to have her innocence proven.

Erin refused to leave her side the entire time. The stylist was out cold on the sofa now. She'd been fine to drive home, so she said, but Layla wanted to keep her friends close. Yes, she was paranoid but her security system gave her some of the safety she craved. The new man Leo Vukovich had stationed in the lobby provided the rest. Russ would have been better but she wasn't going down that road.

She'd spent most of the night on the phone with Martine Peeples. Layla hated to bother the woman and her girlfriend at home but damage control was paramount. At least this time she was on the right side of the law. The press ate up stalker stories, especially ones with happy endings. Too many people knew about the story to hide it, so Layla's best bet was to work it as best she could. She conferenced her agent in on the three-way call and eventually left it to them to work out. She'd play whatever part was assigned.

Both Leo and Russ had texted during the call. Russ sent a simple "glad you're okay" response. Leo sent updates on what charges the police were filing against Bowen and Olson. He also told her there might be charges pending against him. Layla hit the roof.

"He was trying to break into my trailer. My trailer where my sister was hiding. He had a gun. You were defending us. Tell me who to talk to because this shit will not stand."

Leo laughed at her. "I appreciate the defense but it's not going to be a problem. I'll let you know if we need you, okay?"

"Okay." She didn't entirely believe him. Something was going on. Something had happened in the minutes between her dash past the Vukovich boys and the cops showing up. Something bad. In each of his texts, Leo specified that Russ was okay and was handling the situation well. He made a point of it and Layla didn't understand why.

She fell asleep wondering and the world spun on. She woke up in the morning and had an entire day of filming left.

"Coffee?" Kristin begged as she stumbled into the kitchen.

"Tea?"

Her little sister growled. "Coffee. I know you have it."

Kristin off caffeine was officially scarier than the memories of Russ. Layla dragged a stool over to the fridge, reached into the cupboard above it and pulled the canister out from behind the cookbooks.

"I'm never going to laugh at zombie kits again," Erin announced as she bounced into the kitchen. She snagged a cup off the mug tree on the counter and set it beside the one Kristin was filling.

"Zombie kits?"

"Bug out bags? Go bags?"

Layla and Kristin shook their heads, still not following.

"You're supposed to keep a bag in the trunk of your vehicle with a couple changes of clothes and all your essentials. Then in the event of a zombie attack you can grab it and run for the hills without having to go home first," Erin explained.

"That is so cool!" Evidently Kristin's coffee worked quickly. "I should have one of those."

"You really should," Erin agreed. "I don't have to make the trek back to my apartment for fresh clothes before going to work. It would have only made me three hours late."

"We're all going to be late if we don't get going." Layla filled her travel mug with hot water and dropped in a lemon wedge. She wasn't ready for coffee yet.

The lot was a zoo. Layla didn't recognize any of the guards at the gate when they demanded identification from both her and Kristin. Her trailer had yet another new door. The repair crew had added a new frame this time as well.

Everybody on the show seemed to drop in throughout the day. She and Kristin and Erin were a different type of celebrity. She didn't want it. None of it. All Layla wanted in the world was to finish the day and go home and sleep. Maybe when she woke up in the morning the last couple weeks would have been a nightmare. Maybe Russ wouldn't hate her and she wouldn't have felonious stalkers. While she was dreaming, having her entire family back and intact would be nice.

She tried but she couldn't maintain the level of upbeat positivity she'd been showing for the last month or two. She sensed the disappointment at her instinctive attempt to distance herself from everyone but didn't have the energy to explain the reasons behind it. She offered "exhausted" and "freaked out" as excuses and worked her tail off at keeping the bitch queen under wraps. Cool and traumatized were more acceptable than rude every day of the week.

At the end of the day, Layla realized her count was off. One person hadn't stopped by. She knew he was around; she'd seen him.

She'd asked for professional but this was ridiculous. He'd saved her. Her and Kristin and Erin. She should be able to thank him in person for that. Eventually, she tracked him to a corner of the soundstage, the corner she usually chose to disappear to between takes.

The crew worked around him, prepping for a scene she wasn't in. Russ' dark clothes blended into the shadows but nobody went near him. "Stay the fuck away" vibes radiated off him for miles.

Layla ignored them. "Hey."

*

"Hey," a soft, feminine voice whispered. Russ knew she was coming up behind him. He always knew where she was. One word from her was all it took for his heart to start racing.

"Hey."

"I thought I'd see you today."

"I was busy. Work stuff."

Russ watched the top of her head bob up and down. "That was the agreement. Of course, when you save my life in the course of doing your job, I thought it would be appropriate to say thank you in person if it wasn't too inconvenient. If it is, I can leave."

He heard her talking to him, and the edge of pain in her voice. Mostly, though, he heard himself saying how wrong she'd been to protect her little sister. He heard him telling her that the truth was the most important thing, even more important than justice. And he heard himself the night before giving his statement and saying nothing of the timing that would allow Leo to fire his gun, drop it and have Tom pick it up in the second it took him to turn from Bowen to Olson.

"Wow. Okay, then. Good-bye, Russ." The hard soles of her shoes scratched the concrete as she spun around to leave. He caught her arm.

"Don't go."

"You obviously don't want me around. That's what I asked for. I get it. I won't make this mistake again."

"Don't go," he repeated.

"How can I stay?"

"There are things I want to say to you. Need to say. Can I see you later?"

"I think we've said it all."

"No, we haven't. We definitely haven't," Russ insisted. "Please. Ten minutes. Five. Wherever you want. Your trailer?"

"No. My apartment. I'll let them know you'll be there at eight."

"Absolutely."

She stared at the hand that was wrapped around her elbow, then back to his face. Russ peeled his fingers away and fought not to grab at her again. He made a mistake in letting her walk away the first time. Watching her do it again, even for an afternoon, gutted him. The thought it could be the last time ever nearly brought him to his knees.

Russ patted his jacket pocket. If he was doing this, he was going all the way. He had enough time to deliver his resignation letter in person. One thing was clear; it was time to move on from Olympus. Protecting Layla felt right and there were plenty of others that needed him. The rich and famous would pay the bills but he wanted to help people like her—good people in bad places that needed somebody to watch their backs.

Layla had been right, back at the beginning. He was good at fight co-ordination but it wasn't him. Protecting was what he was meant to do. She'd given him the clarity to see that.

Now he prayed that she could see the truth in his next move.

Chapter 22

Layla contemplated opening the bottle of merlot for about a second. The temporary boost of courage wasn't worth the uncontrollable tendency to blurt out whatever was on her mind. Russ didn't deserve to know how much she was hurting without him. If there was anything she could do to get him back, she would but turning back the clock was beyond even the character she played. The refrigerator light glinted off the tinfoil covered cork, urging her to reconsider. She nearly did. Damn those red grapes. The display on her DVR flipped to 7:59 p.m. and her intercom buzzed. He didn't even give her the last minute to work her nerves up to a complete frenzy.

She knew he was on his way up and jumped at the knock anyway. Layla opened the door and was swamped by the huge bouquet of black-eyed Susans in Russ's arms which he shoved in her direction.

"What is this?" she asked.

"Part one of my apology."

"You have a multi-part apology?"

Russ brushed the starched shirt sleeve over his brow. Layla couldn't help but notice the sheen of sweat on his face. "Are you okay?"

"That will depend on you. Can I come in?"

She stepped aside and he stepped through all her defenses. This was such a bad idea. She shouldn't have agreed to this in exchange for the opportunity to thank him. He didn't want her thanks or her friendship. He didn't want her, period. Why was she torturing herself like this?

Layla kept an eye on him while she filled a vase in the kitchen sink. He seemed to be favoring his left leg while he checked out the sunset from her patio doors.

"Are you alright?"

"What?"

"You're limping. Did you get hurt when you stopped Jeremy?"

He gave her a funny look and then hobbled over to the sofa. Layla wasn't certain but he seemed to be protecting his right leg on for those half dozen steps. "I tackled him. I guess the landing was a little rougher than I thought."

Another thing she owed him. Great. Layla grabbed a cushion off the chair seat and put it on the table. "Lift your leg," she said, "and I'll go get you some ice."

She wasn't expecting him to pull her down beside him. "Sit," he ordered. "I need to talk to you."

She tried to pull away. A little. It was awfully comfortable sitting that close though, leaned against his warm side, pressed thigh to thigh. She couldn't help but notice that he smelled of fresh laundry soap and sunshine.

"I fucked up with you," Russ continued.

They were back there again. Why didn't he get out the salt and rub it into her open emotional wound while he was at it? "You've made that clear." Layla tried to stand but the arm around her waist was an iron band.

"I was wrong to judge what you did to protect your sister. I had no right at all to say anything, especially since I wasn't there. I hurt you and I'm sorry," he whispered in her ear.

She sat, frozen. He wasn't supposed to do that—apologize. He wasn't supposed to care anymore because she might care back. It meant she could give him a second chance, if she wanted to. Of course, she wanted to. Everything jumbled in her head and the only way she could express her thoughts was with a tear that made its way halfway down her cheek before she scrubbed it away. "What happened?"

"I don't understand."

"What changed? Why are you sorry now?"

"Can't you just accept my apology?" Russ traced the tear's path with his fingertip.

"It doesn't mean anything unless I can be certain you're not going to turn on me again."

"Layla, I won't. Honest."

"Honest?" Did she have any honesty left in her at this point? Maybe she had enough for one more go-around. "Honestly, I've been half in love with you for almost two years and I fell completely a couple months ago. You're always there, taking care of things. Of me. I trusted that. Even when I was a bitch you were there. I didn't have a chance. For a moment, I thought you felt the same way and I was safe and happy for the first time in ages and then you took it away. You took it back because of something that happened before I even knew you. So yeah, I need to be sure."

"Sweetheart," he began. And stopped.

Her heart broke all over again.

"I lied. For Tom."

His brother? "I don't understand."

"When we went after Bowen, Tom ended up with the gun. Leo told the police that he pulled the trigger. It was Tom. I didn't correct Leo's statement. I didn't say anything. I stayed silent to protect my brother, exactly like you did to protect your sister. The only difference is that nobody innocent got hurt when I did it. To be honest, since we are, I don't think that anything would have made a difference. Leo would have still taken the blame. So how can I tell you that what you did was wrong when I was willing to do the same thing?"

"You lied. You?"

"Yeah, but first I fell in love with a woman who did a good thing and was punished for it and I was arrogant enough to think I could punish her for it again. Then I lied to her, and to the police, and to myself. But if she forgives me, I promise to be honest with her from now on."

Layla had never wanted anything so much in her life.

Russ lowered his head until his forehead rested against hers. "Please, Layla. Some people need a second second chance."

Layla had her three strike rule for a good reason. She'd trusted her parents and Joy over and over again and they'd let her down every time. Kristin, too, although the risk there might finally be rewarded. Maybe lightning could strike twice.

"Some people get them."

* * * *

Fuck, the bitch was back. Russ hid his grin when Layla stomped into her trailer and disappeared to the back room. They were shooting the second to last episode of the season and it was not a pleasant one. Layla was doing her damnedest to play nice with the other kids but her grip was slipping. Russ had been trying all kinds of things to reduce her tension at night. Layla admitted that she was enjoying them but that they weren't helping on the set.

He'd settled into the shadows while she prepped for her last scene of the season with Sean. Hera and Eros had another fight sequence. The other characters were beating the hell out of his girlfriend and it was wearing on more than just Layla. Sean had come to him, concerned, about the intensity of the scenes and there hadn't been anything Russ could do about them except work with the actors to ensure his girlfriend suffered as little bruising as possible.

Sean commented that this episode was written by the same guy who had written the last "toss Hera around" script. Russ made a note for whoever replaced him to keep an eye open for future scripts by this guy and plan the training sessions accordingly. He was grateful to overhear Sean, Nick and Chris commenting on the same thing among themselves. He could trust them to keep an eye on Layla when he was gone.

Layla and Sean had struck up a strange kind of friendship in the last couple months. Nothing romantic – Sean's crush on his on-screen lover was too intense for that. Unfortunately for the god of love, the object of his affection wasn't giving him the time of day.

Russ didn't know how he was going to handle his new job. He knew he could handle the professional aspects of it but not seeing Layla every day was going to be a blow. She needed somebody to watch over her and business at Pacific Personal Security was picking up. Jeremy Bowen was a fading memory but her family was still causing trouble.

He'd thought she was going to break when Kristin called to tell her that her parents had let Joy move back into the house and had returned her car and credit cards. Layla told him that she'd expected it but the news still hit her like a blow.

"Nothing's changed," Layla sobbed. "Joy is going to hurt somebody."

"Not. Your. Fault. You can't control her," Russ repeated endlessly. "You got out. Kristin got out. Concentrate on that."

"But she's my sister."

"I know."

So he held Layla while she cried and wondered if a family so fractured could ever heal. The only bright spot for her was the fact that she was closer than ever to Kristin, who had temporarily moved in with Layla. Having her in the apartment cut significantly into his and Layla's time alone but he didn't mind too much as long as they all continued to respect each other's privacy.

If Russ couldn't protect her from the rest of her family, he could at least offer her a shoulder to cry on even as her tears killed him. Layla could break his heart any time she wanted to, which was only fair since he'd broken hers. He trusted she wouldn't. They were beyond that now. Two months into his last chance and Russ knew that he wasn't going anywhere. Ever.

* * * *

"What are you grinning about?" Layla asked, her toga replaced with her street clothes. She wore a bright red blouse with her jeans. She wore red often after he'd slipped and called her a firecracker to her face. He liked it.

So many ways to answer that. So many ways to get his ass kicked. He settled on, "You've had a hell of a season. I'm going to miss this next year." It had been convenient as hell to meet in her trailer after work and decide whose place they were going to after work. A couple of times they hadn't left the trailer at all.

"I'm going to miss you too." She pushed him back into the sofa cushions and straddled his legs. "But I guess we can go twice as hard in the evenings."

"That might kill us."

Layla leaned into him and whispered, "I'll give it a shot." Then her lips touched his and she got lost in his kiss. Unfortunately, somebody knocked on the door before he got her bra unhooked underneath her shirt.

"Layla? It's me!" Kristin yelled through the locked door.

"Go away!"

"Quit making out with your boyfriend. It's work time. They need you in Wardrobe."

Russ groaned. "I'm really not impressed with your sister's new work ethic. Can't she slack off for once?"

"I wish."

He wrapped his hands firmly around her waist. "Come over to my place tonight."

"My bed is nicer."

"My place," he insisted. "I bought you a big bouquet of daisies."

"I like daisies."

"I know." He'd bought her more than that. He had six bottles of champagne chilling in his fridge, a dozen of their friends coming over, and a small blue box in his wall safe. Layla knew about the box. She didn't know about the timing. Originally he planned to wait until the filming hiatus but he wasn't willing to wait any longer. She didn't have a clue.

He could act too.

The End

Hollywood to Olympus

Screen Idol
Drama Queen
Leading Man
It Girl
Action Hero (coming soon)

Publisher's Note

Please help this author's career by posting an honest
review wherever you purchased this book.

About Elle Rush

Elle Rush is a Canadian romance author from Winnipeg, Manitoba. When she's not travelling, she's hard at work writing her contemporary romance eBooks which are set all over the world. Elle earned a degree in Spanish and French, barely passed German, and is starting to learn Italian and Filipino. She has flunked poetry in every language she's ever taken. She also has mild addictions to tea, cookbooks and the sci-fi channel. Keep up with her new releases by subscribing to her newsletter at www.ellerush.com/newsletter.